ILL WILL

ILL WILL

A Novel

———

EDMUND
DOLLINGER

Full Court Press
Englewood Cliffs, New Jersey

Published in the United States of America
by Full Court Press, 601 Palisade Avenue,
Englewood Cliffs, NJ 07632
fullcourtpress.com

ISBN 978-1-946989-25-3
Library of Congress Catalog No. 2018968297

Editing and book design by Barry Sheinkopf

To my children
Mike, Lanie, Jeff, and Holly
AND MY GRANDCHILDREN
Eric, Jack, and Leah
I love you all

ACKNOWLEDGMENTS

I would like to thank my writing mentor, Barry Sheinkopf, at The Writing Center, for patiently teaching me how to turn a story idea into a completed novel. I couldn't have done it without you.

Thanks also to my Wednesday night writing group, classmates, and critics who listened patiently to and criticized bits and pieces of this book over a number of years—Eugenia Koukounas, Gail Larkin, Edie Messer, Rita Kornfeld, Ora Melamed, Harold Steinbach, Natalie Beaumont, Bill Paladino, Tony Wiersielis, and anyone else I've inadvertently left out.

Thanks also to my cousin, Arlene Pollack, for reviewing my final draft.

Finally, my thanks to the excellent faculty, past and present, of New York University School of Law, for providing my hero Elkins and his author, with an outstanding legal education.

CHAPTER
ONE

H E GASPED AS HE ROLLED OFF HER. "That was great. How was it for you?" It was not the most original of sentiments, but originality was neither of their strong suits.

"I'm not there yet," Alice replied as she bent her knees, spread her thighs, and grasped the back of his head.

He complied; five minutes later, she screamed her release. She rolled over to the left side of her king-sized bed, shook two cigarettes from a pack on the glass-topped night table, lit them with a Zippo lighter, passed one to him, and moved an onyx ashtray to the middle of the bed between them. "That's what I like about you, Lester."

"What?"

"You're not squeamish, and you know how to please a lady."

He took a drag and inhaled deeply. "That's because I have good taste in ladies—especially ones who taste good."

She smiled as they lay back and finished their cigarettes in a leisurely fashion.

Alice rose first and went to the bathroom to sponge herself off. "Want some coffee?" she asked when she returned.

He nodded and padded off to the bathroom. Several minutes later, he was dressed and seated on the living room couch. She brought in two mugs and a plate of cookies. "What was the occasion for inviting me over in the middle of the week?" he asked, taking a sip.

"Can't a girl just want some recreation?" she replied, nibbling a chocolate-chip cookie.

"Not Jim McGrath's niece Alice Keller, all business during the week."

"Well, there *was* something I wanted to talk to you about."

His smile broadened. "I thought so."

"It's Uncle Jim."

"Is he okay?"

She shook her head. "He's had a heart attack and a stroke. He's in a coma. If I had the right paperwork, I'd have the hospital pull the plug."

"Gee, I'm sorry to hear that. How can I help?"

She handed him two unsigned sheets of paper.

He read them and looked up. "What's this supposed to be?"

"The will he signed at Moira's last birthday party two years ago that you and Jack witnessed."

He whistled. "You're a cold bitch. . . . But that's what I like about you. What can we do for you?"

"You know people who can write and sign just like Uncle Jim."

He pursed his lips. "And Jack and I can re-sign and back date it."

She nodded.

"What do we get for it?"

"Tonight was sort of a down payment."

He laughed. "Sweetie, you're a great lay, but this is business. How big is the estate?"

"So who's Alice Keller?" my wife Helen demanded as I trudged into the apartment having spent my day in a hot landlord and tenant court with a broken air conditioner.

"Who told you about her, Rosie?"

Helen nodded.

I bristled. "Doesn't our receptionist have enough to do without calling everybody's wife?"

Helen shook her head. "I called her. I wanted you to know I'd be home from work a little late, but you didn't need the message." She pointed to the kitchen clock that read seven-thirty.

"Well, you know the law's a jealous mistress."

"More jealous than Alice?" she snickered.

"She could be a great piece of business. She works for her uncle, James McGrath, a big slumlord. He just died, and his will leaves everything to her. She wants me to represent the estate."

The cash-register in Helen's eyes started spinning. "How big?"

"Might be over twenty million."

"Wow! That could be a great fee. How'd she get to you?"

"She heard about Ludlow." That was an estate where I'd uncovered a fraud and got a reputation as a hot-shot estates lawyer.

"That's the third referral you've gotten from that case," she said as I returned to the kitchen with a scotch for me and a white wine for her. "Maybe we'll get rich."

"It's not that easy." I continued, taking a slug.

She sipped her wine. "It never is. What's the problem?"

"It's not a lawyer-drawn will, and the witnesses are the boyfriends of the beneficiaries."

Helen nodded. She was an estates paralegal at a mid-sized law firm. We'd met when I worked for the Bronx Surrogate's Court. "You going to take the case?" She filled two plates with veal stew and put them on the breakfast bar we always ate at.

"We're not that far along. She wants to have a meeting at her apartment."

Helen rubbed two fingers together, then broke into a laugh. "House calls?"

"It's worse than that. She lives in one of her uncle's buildings on Hoe Avenue in the Bronx. That's one rough neighborhood—drugs and street gangs. Mark, thinks I should press her to come to the office. He says lawyers don't make house calls."

"Your boss has a point—but will she?"

"She absolutely refused. I told her I'd call her on Monday."

"Why don't you ask Daddy?" Helen's father, Sam Kaplan, was an accountant who grew up in the East Bronx and had many clients there. "We're having dinner with my folks tomorrow."

"Good idea," I replied lifting my fork. "Sam's got a good head on his shoulders."

CHAPTER TWO

F OR CHRISSAKE, CAROL, TURN UP the damned air-conditioner. I'm being boiled alive!" The six-foot four-inch ex-pro linebacker again mopped his sweating brow with an oversized blue-checked handkerchief. During his playing career, Harold McGrath had been a rock-hard 260, but since retirement he'd ballooned eighty pounds, mostly flab.

"The unit needs recharging, dear," replied his petite spouse, who hadn't lost her model's figure—if anything, she was even thinner, but her pretty face had grown hawk-like. "I called the contractor, but with this heat wave, he won't be able to come till Thursday. We really should have had it serviced before the summer season."

"Well, why the hell didn't you?"

"Because you're a cheapskate!"

"What the fuck are you talking about?"

"Remember last winter, when you told me to cut expenses so you'd have enough to go into that downtown real estate deal with Hendricks?"

He glared at her. "That's a lot of crap. I only meant stuff like those two-thousand-dollar dresses you're always buying at Neiman Marcus—not *necessaries*."

"Like your new golf clubs?" she sneered. "Anyhow, it's not working *that* bad. *I'm* not too hot, and you wouldn't be either, if you'd lose some weight."

"Jesus *Christ*, you're a pain in the ass," he grumbled, heading for the door.

"Harold, I wish you wouldn't take the Lord's name in vain," she called after him, hands planted firmly on her narrow hips. "Where are you going?"

"To Scully's, for some cold ones. At least *their* air-conditioning works."

"When'll you be back?" He left without answering.

WHEN HE RETURNED SEVERAL HOURS LATER, she was in her bent ash rocker, sipping a second vodka and tonic and gazing at the setting sun over Charleston harbor. "My don't you look appetizing," she said.

"What do you want?"

"How come you're back? Did you drink Scully's dry?"

"I only had a few."

"A few *pitchers*, I'll bet—*now* where are you going?" He had begun to stagger to the archway that led to the bedrooms.

"I'm going to take a nap."

"Not yet. You had a call."

"Who was it?"

"Your niece Alice."

"What's that bitch want?"

"Your brother Jim died. She wants you to come to New York for the funeral."

He tightened up leaning on a dark heavy sideboard as he scratched his nose.

"Are we going to go?"

"Yeah, *I* am. Pack my bag, get me a flight to New York for the morning, and tell the bitch to pick me up at the airport."

"Shall I make hotel reservations for us?"

"What do you mean, 'us'? Who needs *you* there?"

"Well, I was fonder of Jim than you were."

He gave her an incredulous look, then noisily passed wind. "Who said I was *fond* of the old bastard?"

" Why are you going to the funeral, then?"

"*Funeral?. . .* Yeah, I guess I'll go there, too."

She stared at him.

He shook his head. "I must have married you for your looks. Why am I the second richest member of the Mc-

Grath family?"

Her expression grew serious. "Because your brother Jim was richer."

He nodded. "Pack me a big suitcase. I'll be gone for a couple of weeks."

"How come?"

"To protect my brother's property. I can't let her steal *my* inheritance."

"I'll call Charlie for you."

His look was menacing. "Mind your own fucking business," he growled as he trudged towards the bedroom.

"ISN'T THAT MUCH BETTER, MR. GOLD?" asked the youngish looking man attired in a white coat with North Miami Maimonides emblazoned over the left pocket.

The bald man sitting up on his bed with his eves glued on the TV screen grunted.

"Mind if I borrow this?" the orderly asked as he picked up a newspaper, still in its plastic wrapper.

The old man swept his right hand over his night table, knocking over the water pitcher, but gave no response; and the younger man, after cleaning up the new mess, left the room with the paper.

CHARLES MCGRATH WASHED HIS HANDS thoroughly before he left the staff bathroom. It was the third time that week he'd had to change Gold's dirty diaper. He hated the job, but he had to live. He took the *New York Times* into the employee's lunchroom. It was a little early for his break, but he needed it, and at 10:15 in the morning there was usually no one there. He liked to read the paper without having to talk to his stupid co-workers.

The cramped room was, as he had hoped, empty. He laid the paper down on the steel drainboard next to the sink, poured himself a cup of coffee from the machine next to the refrigerator, added cream and three spoonfuls of sugar, seated himself at the window table, and spread out the paper. Extra calories kept him from looking like a scarecrow; Charlie was the only male McGrath who didn't have a weight problem. He skimmed the front page and read the business section with some care. He wished Gold's family subscribed to the *Wall Street Journal*. He'd read the *Journal* when he worked for his brother, but the *Times* was okay and at least it was fresh. Mr. Gold was too senile to read anything, just stared at the TV. Charlie shook his head, wishing he had a few bucks put away so he could follow his own stocks. He looked at his watch. It was half past. Better get back to work, but first his favorite part of the paper. He turned to the obits.

"Holy *shit!*" he shouted. "*Jim's dead!*" He rushed to the pay phone. Alice would need help managing the real estate business. He wondered if she'd spring for the flight from Miami.

THE CONVENT OF THE SACRED HEART, in downtown Houston, had a Spanish look down to the center courtyard that would have been more appropriate for San Antonio. It housed three dozen nuns—the faculty of several Catholic parochial schools—most at the deep end of middle age, several near retirement. Finding women with a vocation was becoming more and more difficult; some of the church schools had been filling in with lay teachers. Sister Mary Elizabeth Curran was one of two exceptions to the rule. She and Sister Bridget were the only members of the order under fifty, and at twenty-seven she was the only one under thirty.

At 4:20 in the afternoon, Mary Elizabeth left the school building at St. Paul's, where she taught first grade. It was the end of May and she'd begun to think about the coming school year. The heat hit her like a blast furnace. She would have liked to remain in the air-conditioning longer, but she had to get back for evening devotions. Over the eight short blocks back to the convent, her white summer habit wilted. She again noticed the cracked stone and peeling plaster on the building and was forcibly reminded of the repairs that had to be made.

In the reception area she found two letters and a telephone message for her. At the pay phone on the wall next to the reception desk she called home.

By the time she replaced the receiver, her pretty face had grown ashen. "What's the matter, Sister?" asked the nearly eighty-year-old nun behind the desk.

"My. . .my uncle from New York just died. My mother wants me to go to the funeral."

The elderly nun nodded sympathetically and picked up her phone. ". . .Mother can see you in her office now, Sister."

As Mary Elizabeth climbed the steep circular staircase to the third level, she wondered how Mother Superior was able to make the climb at least four times daily. At the top of the steps she turned right, reached the end of the open corridor that overlooked the courtyard, and knocked at a distressed wood door. "Come in, dear," a slightly gravely voice called out.

When the young nun entered the nine-foot-square room, a tall, gaunt woman, attired in the heavy black winter robes of her order rose from behind her gray steel desk, crossed in front of the three filing cabinets that stood next to the left hand wall, embraced her young sister, and installed her in a steel visitor's chair.

As she resumed her seat behind her desk, Mary Elizabeth wondered how she could survive in the stifling hot room without window or fan and not even perspire. "Thank you for seeing me so quickly, Mother."

"God's will be done. When did your Uncle James die?"

"Yesterday evening, Mother. My mother asked whether I could go to the funeral."

"Your mother is a good woman. She was one of my students at St. Anthony's, you know, just as you were. Actually, I've known about your uncle for a few hours. Your mother called me this afternoon. There's a flight leaving for New York tomorrow morning at seven. Here are your tickets. There's a branch of our order in Manhattan. I've made arrangements for you to stay there."

"What about my class?"

"We've already called for a substitute until you get back."

Mary Elizabeth was astonished.

"Don't be so surprised, my dear. We do our best to take care of our own."

"Thank you, Mother,"

"Actually," the older one continued, "I do have an ulterior motive. . . . Your mother has spoken to me about your Uncle James over the years. She told me he was a very rich man in real estate."

The young nun nodded.

"She also told me she believed that your uncle had made substantial provisions for our order in his will. While you're in New York, you might be able to make some discreet inquiries. We are, as you know, in sad need of repairs."

CHAPTER THREE

Y THE SECOND MONDAY IN JUNE, the heat had abated a little, but I kept the air-conditioner at full blast as I drove to the East Bronx. I was feeling edgy and having second thoughts about the wisdom of visiting Alice Keller at her apartment. Sam had warned me about the neighborhood, but the estate was too large not to take the risk. At least I had resisted meeting her there after work. The neighborhood was bad enough in daylight. We'd compromised on 4:00 P.M. I left the office at 3:30, drove east on Tremont Avenue, turned south on Boston Road, east on 174th Street under the El, and right onto Hoe Avenue. Parking was tight; I was lucky to find a spot a block away.

When I reached her building, three teenage boys in jeans, Nikes, and tee shirts with pictures of a Great White Shark were sitting on the stoop. "Where you goin', man?" asked the biggest and darkest of the three. He had two gold rings in each of his nostrils.

"I'm here to see Alice Keller."

"Oh, da super," said a lighter-skinned boy with a large gold earring in each ear. "What you want with her?"

"I have an appointment."

"'Bout what?" asked the third boy, devoid of visible jewelry.

"Hey—get the fuck *out* of here!" came a voice from inside the front door, which was opened by a blonde woman in her thirties dressed in a short jean skirt and white golf shirt.

The boys grumbled but left.

"You Mr. Elkins?"

I nodded.

"I'm Alice Keller. Come on in." She was about five-feet-six, stocky but not fat, with protruding breasts unhampered by a bra, and muscular legs. Her face was pleasant but not pretty. She led me into the building through a clean, well-lighted hallway, past the staircase to the upper floors, and through a doorway at the end of the hall. The cool air as I entered the apartment surprised me. Rent controlled buildings in the East Bronx rarely had adequate wiring for air conditioning. The front door led directly into a tastefully furnished, carpeted living room, and she motioned me to a love seat facing a 21-inch T.V along the right-hand wall. "Can I offer you a cold drink?" she asked, pointing to a glass on the cocktail table in front of me. "I'm drinking iced coffee."

"Thank you. That'd be fine."

"Milk, sugar, Sweet 'n Low?" she asked, turning towards the kitchen.

"Just a little milk, please."

She returned a minute later with my drink in a tall glass, placed it on the table in front of me, and seated herself in an armchair to my left.

"When did your uncle die?" I asked, taking a pad out of my briefcase.

"Two weeks ago. The funeral was a week ago Saturday."

"Was he ill long?"

"No, it was a stroke and massive heart attack. I didn't even know he had a serious heart problem."

"I thought so. I saw him in court in April, and he looked his usual vigorous self."

"I thought you were an estates lawyer," she said, concerned.

"I am, but my firm is too small for me to do just one thing. I handle all the estates in the office, but I do the landlord-and-tenant and a few other things, too. I've had four or five cases against your uncle. He was one tough guy."

She smiled. "Uncle Jim was a pussycat, but he could look and talk mean. He said he had to in order to keep up his reputation."

I chuckled and took a sip of my coffee. "You told me the will was home drawn."

"Yes. Want to see it?"

I nodded. She left the room and returned with a red legal file, from which she withdrew two sheets of paper. "That's it, I typed it myself."

"How come he didn't go to a lawyer? He was in business."

She shrugged. "Beats me. I asked him to, but he said it was a simple will and didn't need one."

"With his real-estate business, didn't he have a lawyer on retainer? Max Cohen always represents him in landlord and tenant court. The firm is Cohen and Finkelstein, isn't it?"

She nodded. "He didn't want them to. Said it was 'none of their goddamn business.'"

"Did you ask them if they ever drew a will for your uncle?"

She scratched the underside of her right knee. "I didn't bother. Max Cohen doesn't know about anything except landlord- and-tenant, and Izzy Finkelstein's been retired for a while. I wouldn't know where to find him."

"I'll check with Max. Who's Moira Keller?"

"My sister. She died a few months after the will was signed."

"And the witnesses?"

"Jack Gorman and Lester Smith."

"And they're. . .?"

She scratched her left shoulder with her right hand, her forearm resting on her bosom. "Jack was engaged to my sister, and Les and I've been going together."

"Where was the will signed?"

She pointed to a dining room table sitting at the far end of the living room adjoining the kitchen.

"Who else was present?"

"Uh—just Moira and me. It was her birthday, and Uncle Jim came over to celebrate with us."

"And you planned his will signing for the same time?"

She frowned. "I didn't plan anything. We didn't know anything about it before he came over."

I was puzzled. "I thought you typed it."

"I did. We were supposed to get together at four and eat at five or six, but Uncle Jim came at one. We had a drink together and he told me he wanted to have a will and leave everything to Moira and me. I told him to see his lawyer, but he refused. Then he pulls this form out of an envelope." She pointed to the will in Ian's hands.

"And?"

"And told me what to type. We had a few more drinks, and when Les and Jack came over, they signed it."

"HE MUST HAVE BEEN SLOSHED TO THE EARS when he signed that will." Mark Rooney was leaning back in his chair, heels on the right writing pullout and sipping a highly sweetened iced cappuccino, his favorite summer drink. It was Tuesday afternoon, and he had insisted on seeing me as soon as I returned from court.

"Not according to Alice. She says he could drink glassfuls of Black Bush all day and not feel a thing."

"A real hollow leg, huh? Not like those creeps you see marching in the St. Paddy's Day parade." Rooney took a bite of his jelly donut, returned it to the paper plate on his left, and licked the powdered sugar from his fingers.

I glanced furtively at my boss's protruding belly, and wondered if Kathy Rooney was on his case the same way Helen was about mine.

"What about the two brothers and the sister? Aren't they going to object?"

"Alice says no. Harold McGrath is a blowhard. . . . She says he made some noise about his share of the estate at the wake, but he won't do anything. He's an ex-pro football player, and he has quite a few bucks, but he's too cheap to spend money on a lawyer. When he was a player, they lowballed his salary because he was too tight to use an agent."

Rooney took another sip of his drink. "What about the other brother?"

"Charlie's a stupid wimp, according to her. He used to work for Jim, helped to manage his buildings—basically the same job Alice had before his death. Alice'd just finished college and was working as Charlie's assistant. She found out he was getting petty graft from some of the suppliers and leaked it to Jim, who fired him. Now Charlie's working as an orderly in a nursing home in Florida. She paid for his airfare to the funeral. He asked her for a job, and she promised him one after the will's probated."

Rooney shrugged and took another bite of donut. "How about the sister?"

"She's a widow. Her daughter's a nun down in Texas. She won't fight."

Rooney laughed. "Don't be so sure. You don't know the Church. So she definitely wants to retain us?"

"Yup."

"Did you discuss our fee?"

"Yeah. I told her five percent of the gross was the

norm, but it was way too high for a twenty million dollar estate. I offered to take two and a half, and she jumped at it. "

Rooney frowned. "Why didn't you let her react to the five? She might have agreed to it."

I shook my head. I knew my ethical reasoning wouldn't

work with. "Look, Mark, there'll be a federal estate tax audit, and the IRS will disallow it. Then we'll have a fee fight with the client, and the surrogate will know we're being pigs and cut us way down. I think the two-and-a-half is a fair fee, and it'll fly."

The frown turned to a grin. "Then it's a great deal—*if* we don't have to litigate."

"I told her that the contingency fee didn't include a contested probate or other litigation, and she agreed to pay us our usual rate for the litigation."

"Ian, my boy, you did very well. Write up the retainer, show it to me, and get it signed as quick as you can."

I nodded.

Rooney's face darkened again. "You sure she can afford the freight for the litigation?"

"I guess she can. I couldn't *ask*, could I?"

Rooney shook his head and wiped some powdered sugar from his lips. "It's a chancy business. But I wouldn't have done it any different."

"ONLY ONE LITTLE PIECE? What's the matter, it's not good?"

"It's super, Mom. Really it is, but if I have another piece I won't be able to fit into my pants."

"Mom, one's more than enough for him," Helen chimed in. "I don't need a fat husband."

"Don't be silly. *Eric's* had two pieces," Molly replied, looking at her painfully thin, curly-haired other son-in-law, who was Sam's junior partner.

"That's not fair, Mom," said Betty Goldstein, Molly's older daughter, a near carbon copy of her mother down to the striking chestnut hair that Molly was now maintaining from a bottle. "You know my husband has the metabolism of a teenager. He could eat the whole damned cake and never gain an ounce," she concluded with a glance at the huge ice cream cake in the middle of the dining room table, emblazoned with the motto *Happy Anniversary Betty and Eric.*

"I could use a little more," said Sam. "Just so it wouldn't go to waste."

"Remember what the doctor said!" Molly shook her head sadly.

"But it's going to melt."

"Look, Mom, I've got a good idea," Eric suggested. "Put it in the freezer now. That way you can feed it to Freddie and fatten him up before he goes away to camp."

With a smile, she picked up the cake and carried it into the kitchen.

"Who's for some cognac in their coffee?" Sam asked. "I just opened a new bottle of Martel."

"Not for me, Dad," replied Eric. "Tomorrow's a work day."

"Same here," I said. "I've got to drive home."

"How'd you make out on the big estate?"

I told them about it, but when I got to the fee, Eric jumped all over me.

"Are you out of your mind. You just gave away a-half-million bucks." He turned to Helen. "Divorce your Boy Scout before he puts you on welfare."

I gritted my teeth. "Look Eric, I'm a professional. I don't cheat my clients. I don't have a license to steal."

Eric laughed derisively, but Sam held up his hand. "He's right. The IRS will never let him get away with five. Two-and-a-half is a damned good fee."

"Not if the family fights the will," Eric replied.

"The fee doesn't include litigation. She'll have to pay our time charges and give us a retainer."

"Does she have it?"

"Mark's worried about that, too."

"That Irishman you work for is no dummy," Sam remarked as he took another sip of coffee, "but he's more of a crap-shooter than I'd be comfortable with."

CHAPTER FOUR

WHATEVER ALICE THOUGHT, Harold McGrath took immediate action when he was served with probate papers. On July 5, he flew to New York, drove to White Plains, parked his rented green Impala in the municipal garage and waddled four long blocks, past the new courthouse under construction, to a ten story white office building. When he entered, he was bathed in sweat and almost gasping for breath. Carol's right, he thought—he had to lose some weight. The lobby was stark and plainly decorated, with white walls and a bank of four elevators at the far end, and empty except for a uniformed security guard behind a counter along the left wall. "Where's the surrogate's court?"

"Eighth floor. Please sign in," the guard replied, pointing to an open book on the counter.

As Harold did so, he noticed the last person for the eighth floor had signed in twenty minutes before—the man Harold was supposed to meet. "This guy," Harold asked, pointing to the name *Bruce Malone*. "He upstairs?"

The guard shrugged, and Harold turned to the elevators. On eight he turned right and entered the clerk's office. It was at least thirty feet square, with a carpeted floor. There was a center aisle, with counters on each side, that ended in a wall along which stood the offices of the various clerks. The one on the right turned at right angles across from several coin-operated copying machines. Harold spotted a painfully thin man over six five, with a square black beard covering the point of his chin, leaning against one of the copiers He was dressed in chinos and a tee-shirt with a picture of a magnifying glass and the legend *Malone Disputed Documents*.

"Mr. Malone?" Harold asked.

"How'd you guess?" the other replied, and both men chuckled. "Did you bring the exemplars?"

Harold opened his wafer-thin attaché case, removed a small envelope, and handed it to the expert, who spread out the sparse contents on the copier—two postcards, and a few short letters. "It's all I could find," Harold said with a shrug.

"A little skimpy, but it'll do. At least this letter has flow and a full signature."

Harold smiled.

"He sure didn't like you," Malone continued cheerfully.

"We had our differences," Harold replied, the smile turning into a frown.

"Sure did," Malone persisted. "'I'll sue you for slander.' We can probably subpoena a better example for the trial," he concluded. "Let's do the comparison."

Malone picked up the papers and a square case, and led Harold to the counter. After waiting a few minutes, a clerk took their order and brought out the original will. The expert opened the case and removed a machine that had a flat-glass bed with lights under it and a magnifier above. He placed it on the counter and plugged it into an outlet on the floor. Then he laid the will on one side and moved the exemplars around next to it. After several minutes he unplugged the machine, took the will to one of the copiers, made three copies, and returned it to the clerk.

"Well?" Harold asked.

"A forgery—and a pretty crappy job."

At 4:00 in the afternoon, my intercom buzzed. "Yes, Rosie."

"Mr. Rooney is available to see you now, Mr. Elkins. I'm bringing him coffee and some goodies. Can I get you something?"

"Coffee with milk and no sugar would be great, but skip the goodies for me."

"Mrs. Elkins put you on a diet?"

"I'm trying to watch what I eat. My pants are feeling a trifle snug."

Five minutes later, I was seated in one of the great man's visitor's chairs, sipping from a container. Rooney was leaning forward, munching on the first of three chocolate-covered donuts resting on a paper plate. To the right of the plate was a mug of coffee with the legend *Boss* emblazoned on it in red.

"What happened with McGrath?"

"I was served with objections."

"Let's see them."

I handed him a set of backed papers, and Rooney took a swallow of coffee before he leaned back and read.

"Forgery."

I nodded.

"Who's Joe Bennett? Do you know him?"

"I've met him a few times. He used to do some Iron Curtain kinship cases. Appeared before me two or three times when I was a referee."

"Does he know what he's doing?"

"He seemed competent when I was with the court."

". . .But?"

I scratched my chin. "I don't know—he's not handling this the usual way. The experienced guys don't jump in that quick."

Rooney leaned forward, took another bite of donut, and fixed me with a puzzled stare. "What do you mean?"

"He's not using the pre-objection rules to get an edge. He's entitled to a 1404 examination before he files objections."

"Greek to me, son."

"Under Rule 1404, you're entitled to examine two subscribing witnesses, the proponent of the will, and the lawyer who drew it before you have to file objections. This can give you an advantage in deciding what to put *into* the objections right up front rather than possibly needing to amend them later, after the depositions are taken. Even better, the examinations are free. The estate has to pay the reporter's fees."

Rooney nodded. "Any idea why he didn't?"

"I was curious about that, and about who his expert was. I tried to ask him when I was served, but he told me to go to hell, that he wouldn't talk to forgers."

"That's strange," Rooney said, taking another sip. "Any guess what's going through his mind?"

"A few. It may be lack of experience. His former firm did a lot of kinship cases, but he may never have handled a probate."

Rooney again shrugged. "Or?"

". . .This one may be coming out of left field."

He smiled. "I think you estates lawyers *live* there. Let's hear it."

"Remember Justin Taylor from the Ludlow Estate?"

"The lawyer on the other side who got disbarred?"

I nodded. "Bennett was in the same firm with Taylor."

"So?"

"So maybe his real agenda was to file his objections fast so he had a better chance to lock up the client."

Rooney laughed. "You're right, you're *way* out in left field. Have you talked to your client?"

I nodded.

"What did she say?"

"She was shocked her uncles would do that, but she agreed to retain us at an hourly rate."

"What about an advance retainer?"

"I told her I needed ten up front. She said she needed a few days to get it."

"Anything else?"

"I told her we should engage a handwriting expert. Herb Crowley's uncle has a good one." Herb, my closest friend, had worked with me in the law department of the Bronx Surrogate's Court.

"Good idea—but hold up till you get the front money."

"No problem. She agreed that we'd need one, but she wants to ask around first."

ON WEDNESDAY NIGHT, ALICE AND LES were sipping coffee and eating slices of a danish ring at her kitchen table recuperating from nearly two hours of sex.

"This is our second midweek romp," he quipped. "Want to make it a tradition?"

"Tonight's a celebration. Didn't you enjoy it?"

"Sure I did. . . How come?"

"Damn it, Lester, you know me too well."

"So? What are we celebrating?"

". . .Remember the problem I was telling you about?"

"The cash flow?"

She nodded and took a big sip of her coffee.

"How'd you *do* that? I thought Chase had shut down all of his accounts as soon as they learned he was dead."

"They did, but Apple Bank's not that smart."

"Isn't that where you have the tenant security accounts? You could get your ass in a lot of trouble."

She smiled. "Yeah, but who's going to know?"

AS I RETURNED FROM COURT two days later, I was again summoned into the great man's lair. It was lunch time, and Rooney was just finishing an extra large meatball hero. "What's up, Mark?"

"You did good, kid." Rooney blotted a spot of sauce from his blue-and-gray rep tie.

"McGrath?"

Rooney nodded, waving a check. "Ten Gs." He handed it to me. "What's the matter?" he asked, noticing my troubled expression.

"I wonder who McGrath Residential, Inc. is."

"Must be one of her uncle's corporations," Rooney replied stuffing the wrapping from his sandwich into a paper bag and dropping it into the waste basket.

"How can we take it? We weren't retained by the *corporation*."

"Look, kid," Rooney sighed, wiping his lips with a napkin that went into the basket, too. "What's the worst that can happen if we take it?"

I thought for a minute, then shrugged.

"If the corporation sues, we'll have to give it back. Right?"

"I guess so," I admitted.

"Well, that's a risk I'll take for money in the bank. What's *bothering* you?"

"I wonder what *this* is," I asked, pointing to a blacked-out half line next to the corporate name.

Rooney shrugged.

"Apple Bank is where a lot of landlords keep their tenant security accounts."

"Don't even think it," the older lawyer replied, shaking his head. "When the check clears, we can order the handwriting expert."

"Nope."

"How come?"

"The client says she was recommended to a good one."

"Do you know him?"

I shrugged. "She'll be calling me in a few days with his name and phone number."

CHAPTER FIVE

OSEPH BENNETT REMEMBERED ME WELL. He'd appeared before me in three Eastern bloc kinship cases, and he believed I had busted his chops in all them, forcing him to put in impeccable proofs. But while law assistants in other counties may have been nowhere near as strict, I believed in doing my job.

At that moment in his day, Bennett was answering the intercom. "The McGraths are here to see you, Mr. Bennett," he heard.

"I'll be with them in a moment, Andrea." He arranged the scattered papers on his desk into a neat stack, put on his jacket, and finger combed his thinning black hair before he strode out.

Hal and Charlie were in the waiting room. Hal's great bulk nearly filling a blue leather love seat; Charlie's lean frame was neatly perched on the edge of a matching easy chair. "Good morning, gentlemen," said Bennett, extending his hand. "It's good meeting you at last. I was a fan of yours when you were with Dallas," he told Hal. "I'll bet the running backs are glad you've retired."

Hal smiled broadly.

Turning toward Charlie, Bennett added, "I presume you're Mr. Charles McGrath. I didn't know I'd have the pleasure of representing you in this case."

"You don't yet."

Bennett pulled at the pointed beard, he'd grown to camouflage a pudgy face. "Please join me in my office." He held open the swinging door, relieved that he had bought a small sofa. Hal would never have fit into one of his visitor's chairs.

"Can I get you some coffee?" he asked after they had seated themselves. They nodded; he pressed the intercom. "Andrea, send me up a coffee service."

Charlie rose from his seat and strolled around the room. He stopped to look at a group of Picasso and Chagall reproductions on the rear wall, returned to Bennett's desk, and peered at several diplomas behind him. "I thought all you lawyers went to Harvard."

"No, Mr. McGrath, some of us went to other schools.

If every lawyer went to Harvard, there'd be no room there," Bennett concluded with a straight face. "But you'll notice that I went to Boston College. That's right next door."

Charlie was about to continue his examination when Hal barked, "Sit the hell down." His brother obeyed. "What's going on with the case?" Hal asked.

"I filed objections to the will. I sent you a copy."

"I saw them. What're you going to do *now*?"

"I don't think we should be discussing strategy in front of your brother if I don't represent him."

"Why not?" Charlie asked. "I want to see what you're about before I decide to retain you, or even if I'm going to attack the will."

Bennett smiled. The guy wasn't as stupid as his brother made him out to be. "There's a very good reason, Mr. Mc-Grath. If I don't represent you, what we say wouldn't be confidential or covered by attorney-client privilege. I was led to believe that you had told your brother you might not object to the will. Why don't we first discuss why you might be changing your mind?" There was a knock at the door. "Come in, Vickie."

The door opened and a short, chubby, Hispanic woman in a green-and-white maid's outfit entered. She was carrying a tray with a thermal carafe, white china cups and saucers, a jug of milk, and a holder for sugar and artificial sweetener. "You want I should pour, Mr. Bennett?"

"No, thanks," Bennett replied, signed a charge slip, and removed the copy.

He poured the coffee, served his visitors, took a sip himself, and turned to Charlie. "You were about to tell me about your change of heart."

"Yeah, tell us about it," Hal added.

Charlie pinched his nostrils, leaned back in his seat. "It's all about money. I'm not a rich man like my brothers." He lapsed into a long silence while Hal glared at him and the lawyer held himself in check.

"So what the fuck does that mean?" Hal finally asked.

"I was wondering about that, too," Bennett added.

"Look, Mr. Bennett," Charlie began.

"Joe."

"Joe. . . . I always got the short shrift money-wise in this family."

Hal started to interrupt, but the lawyer held up his hand. "He's got to get this out."

Charlie smiled and said to Hal, "You went to college, played pro football, made good bucks. Jim went into real estate and made millions. Look at me. I'm too small for big-time sports, so I couldn't get a college scholarship like you."

"You could have studied harder and gotten an academic one."

"And nobody in the family'd help me," Charlie continued, ignoring his brother's comment.

"Jim gave you a job."

Charlie shrugged. "Some job!"

"You were his *manager*."

"Manager? Shit. I was a fucking *gofer*, and the pay stunk."

"Better than you're getting now," Hal added. "Till Jim fired your ass."

When Charlie snickered, Bennett shook his head at Hal. "Let him finish. . . . So why were you supporting the will?"

"Who says I'm not still supporting it?"

"Sorry."

"Because of this cheap bastard. Alice paid my air fare to the funeral. . . . You didn't even call to tell me Jim died."

"What're you *talking* about? I would have called and taken you along."

"Sure you would've. How come you were shocked to see me at the wake?"

Hal offered no reply, and the lawyer hid his amusement by sipping coffee.

"And Alice offered me a job."

"So take it," Hal replied, a grin contorting his fat face.

"Maybe I will, after she probates the will."

"Why not now?" Hal asked, continuing to smile. "Cause there's no offer unless you support her and she wins."

Charlie's face fell.

"And that means you'd get no share of Jim's twenty mil."

"Look, Hal, I'm willing to jump on your bandwagon, but I can't afford to pay *a lawyer*."

"Who asked you to? I'm laying it out, and when we win, I'll get it back from the estate. Right, counselor?"

Joe nodded.

"So now you're on our side—right?"

Charlie almost nodded. "There *is* something more."

"Yeah?"

"It's awfully tough to live on what they pay at the nursing home. If you could—"

Hal held up his hand. "Mr. Bennett, will you excuse us while my brother and I discuss family matters?"

The lawyer refilled his cup and carried it from the room. Ten minutes later Charlie summoned him back.

"You now have two clients, counselor," said Hal as Bennett resumed his seat.

"Glad to hear it. Welcome aboard, Mr. McGrath."

"Now what was that you were going to tell us about your strategy?" Charlie asked.

Bennett leaned back in his seat. "Do you gentlemen know anything about Ian Elkins?"

"Who's he?" Charlie asked.

"Alice's lawyer, stupid," Hal replied. "What about him?"

"He's a scum bag."

"So? Ain't all of you?"

"That's what a lot of the public thinks," Bennett replied, laughing. "And we're going to use that prejudice to our advantage."

Both McGraths seemed puzzled.

"If you gentlemen were on our jury and Alice were accused of forging Jim's will, would you believe it?"

"Maybe, but ain't it your job to convince us she did?"

The lawyer nodded. "But what if I told you that Alice's scumbag *lawyer* had it forged? Wouldn't you be more inclined to believe it then?"

"Yeah!" said Charlie.

"How're you gone to prove that?" Hal asked.

"Leave it to me. Even if I can't prove it, the accusation will help us with the jury."

When the McGraths left their lawyer's office, they were both cheery.

AT 8:00 THAT EVENING Alice had just finished dinner. She stacked her plate and silverware into the sink, set up the coffee maker for four cups, and turned it on. She was looking forward to a Cary Grant movie on the TV at eight-thirty. God, but that man turned her on. She wondered whether he was as good in the sack as Lester. Probably not. They said he was gay. Then she heard the outside buzzer.

Who the fuck was that? she wondered. She pressed the intercom. "Yes?"

"It's Jack, Alice. Buzz me in."

She did and a moment later the bell rang. She opened her door to a younger version of her Uncle Hal. She wondered how a petite woman like her sister could have put up with him. "How *are* you?" she crooned, presenting her right cheek for the obligatory kiss. "It's so good to see you. Sit down in the living room. I was just making some coffee."

As he did so, she turned to the kitchen to get the coffee, but not before she ripped a paper towel from a roll over the sink and wiped her cheek. Within five minutes she had put up a full pot, set with two mugs of coffee and a plate of cookies on a tray, and carried it into the living room.

"How've you been?" he asked after wolfing down three cookies and a mouthful of coffee.

"Hanging in."

"Better than hanging out."

"*Moi?*" she asked, pointing at herself.

They both laughed.

"To what do I owe the honor of this visit?"

"I've been thinking."

"Really?"

They both laughed again. Jack stuffed four more cookies into his mouth, and Alice returned to the kitchen to refill the plate and check on the coffee. She was glad he hadn't come earlier, remembering how he used to scrounge dinners when Moira was alive.

"What were you thinking about?" she asked as she returned.

"I read Hal's objections."

"Real nasty stuff," she replied.

"It's a good thing you weren't the writer."

"Yeah, but a pity Moira was so sick. I couldn't tell the difference between his handwriting and hers. Your friend, Mario, wasn't near as good."

"Wasn't *that* bad. . . but there's a way around it."

She sipped her coffee. "Oh?"

"Yeah, it was his idea."

"What idea?"

"He thought if we had some samples of Jim's writing that matched the will, it would help."

She stared at her almost-brother-in-law for what seemed an eternity. Then she finished her coffee and took both mugs back to the kitchen. When she returned she sipped the fresh coffee in silence for several minutes.

"What's bugging you, Alice?"

"How much is Mario going to charge? I don't have that much cash available."

"Not to worry, sweetie. He doesn't want any more up front. He was thinking about two-hundred Gs after we win, and he'll testify as our expert."

CHAPTER SIX

A LTHOUGH NAME "ROONEY" SUGGESTS Irish roots, some of his friends and acquaintances believe Mark is really an Englishman. His eating habits certainly support that view. Every afternoon between three and five he becomes ravenously hungry and puts in his order for tea. He drinks coffee instead of tea, and eats cakes, cookies, or donuts instead of scones and small sandwiches, but the timing is there. Perhaps my exposure to his gluttony may be keeping me from completely outgrowing my clothing. On the Wednesday after Labor Day, having devoured half of his four chocolate-covered donuts and consumed his first cup of coffee, Rooney hit the intercom button. "Rose, get me a refill on my coffee."

"Yes, sir."

"And ask Mr. Elkins to join me."

Five minutes later, I was seated in the middle of his three visitor's chairs with a container of coffee in front of me; the great man was drinking his refill from the *Boss* mug.

"What's up?"

"That's what I want to ask *you*," he snapped.

"McGrath?"

"No. Why is the new kid covering your landlord-and-tenant on Friday?"

"McGrath. Judge Carter scheduled a conference for ten."

"What're you, talking settlement?"

"Mark, this is surrogate's court, not supreme. When objections are filed, it's customary for the judge to have a conference to schedule discovery and decide when the case will be ready for trial. Of *course* settlement can come up."

"Who're you going to examine?"

"I don't know yet. I served a demand for a bill of particulars on the objections, but Bennett hasn't responded yet. I suppose I'll examine Hal and Charlie McGrath."

"Who will Bennett examine?"

"I guess Alice and the two witnesses."

"Have you prepped them yet?"

"I haven't even *met* them. I've been pestering Alice for a meeting, but she's been putting me off. I also don't know who our handwriting expert is."

"Keep pressing her, and keep me advised," Rooney replied.

I looked puzzled at my boss.

"Ian, I know you're a good lawyer, but you don't have that much litigation experience. I have, and this is a big case."

I left the room feeling mildly disappointed.

THAT FRIDAY MORNING, A FEW MINUTES AFTER 9:00, I parked in the municipal garage next to the Galeria and had breakfast at the bagel shop just down the block. One of the advantages of being in a court away from the Bronx was that Helen couldn't make me eat a healthy, low-calorie diet. I would never have gotten away with an everything bagel thickly covered with scallion cream cheese at home. Alas, I didn't enjoy such forbidden-fruit breakfast as much as I would have liked. There were knots in my stomach in anticipation of the impending conference. I wondered if I'd ever get over the jitters that came with going in front of a judge I hadn't previously appeared before. Maybe more experience would cure the nervousness, but I doubted it. Mark had told me that all trial lawyers got the shakes; the more experienced ones just knew how to hide it better. With luck I wouldn't get an ulcer.

When I finished, I covered the five long blocks to the surrogate's courthouse. It was a quarter to ten and, as usual, the courtroom was still locked. I looked up at the bulletin board to the left of the door, but the calendar hadn't been posted.

I seated myself on a bench just opposite the door and pulled a back law journal from my brief case. Three minutes later a heavy-set blonde woman joined me on the bench. She pulled a file from a thick attaché case and began to read. We didn't speak.

Five minutes later, the door opened and a court clerk tacked up the calendar. When the woman and I rose, she shouldered her way ahead of me, slowly moved her head down the sheet, frowned, looked up, and smiled. Her case was obviously first. As I approached, another lawyer was peering over my shoulder. I ran my eyes down the list. There were eleven conferences; McGrath was number seven.

The standard-issue courtroom had three windows overlooking the street. I could see bright sunshine through the middle one. Ceiling mounted fluorescents illuminated a center aisle that led to a blonde wood partition between the public seating area and the well of the court. The jury box occupied the left side of the well and contained fourteen seats. The judge's bench was in the center, and on the right sat a desk for the clerk. At the foot of the aisle a swinging door led to the well; the dozen light wooden benches on each side sat six. I seated myself on the left side of the right front bench. The heavy blonde took the far one on the left.

The courtroom soon began to fill, and most of the seats

in the front three rows were occupied in short order. I joined a line of attorneys in front of the clerk's desk. As I signed in, I noticed that my adversary's presence had already been noted. I turned around and saw Joe Bennett seated in the second row. Returning to my seat, I resumed my perusal of the law journal until I was interrupted by a banging of the gavel and the announcement, "All rise. The Surrogate's Court of the State of New York, County of Westchester, is now in session, Honorable Albert Carter presiding."

"Good morning, ladies and gentlemen," said the jowly judge with the graying sandy-blonde hair.

"Good morning, Your Honor," we all called out.

"Conferences will be held in my robing room," the judge concluded as he rose from the bench.

Five minutes later the clerk called the first conference; the blonde and a tall, hawk-nosed brunette disappeared through the doorway.

For the next hour I read back issues of the law journal until I ran out of reading material. I regretted not having packed a few more. I opened the McGrath file, intending to do some prep, but closed it a minute later when I realized that I had it memorized. As another conference was called, I left the courtroom, used the men's room, and phoned the office. Time dragged. Several of the other lawyers were chatting, but I only knew Bennett and am too shy to strike up a conversation with strangers.

Another hour later, the clerk called McGrath.

As I passed through the doorway leading to the robing room, Bennett tried to push past me but was blocked by my protruding hip. In the Elkins world, chivalry does not extend to other men. The court officer knocked at the robing room door and we were told to enter. The judge's rectangular dark-wood desk was backed along the right-hand wall of the ten-foot-square room. To his right were two windows offering an interior view. Behind him stood a set of bookshelves on standards. On one of these, a machine contained a half-full carafe of coffee. There were five plain wooden visitor's chairs. The judge was reading a file, deep in concentration, his mid-sized second chin hanging down over the papers. To his right, a black mug appeared to be full. He looked up as we entered. "Please be seated. Mr. Elkins?"

"Yes, Your Honor," I replied as I sat.

"My colleague Judge Stevens tells me you used to work for Judge McCann."

"Yes, sir."

"Howard was an excellent surrogate—so's George."

I nodded.

"I'm Joseph Bennett, Your Honor."

"Yes, I know. You've made some serious charges in your objections."

"I know, Your Honor."

"You'd better be able to prove them."

"I will."

The judge's expression remained placid. He took a sip of coffee. "What about discovery? Whom will you be examining, Mr. Elkins?"

"The two objectants and their expert—but there is a problem, Your Honor."

"What's that?"

"I served a demand for a bill of particulars on counsel, and he hasn't responded."

"What about it, Mr. Bennett?"

Bennett tugged at the point of his beard. "The demand's excessive."

"Then either move against it or give the particulars. I will expect a motion or a bill to be filed within a week."

"Yes, Your Honor."

"Mr. Elkins, notice your examinations of the McGraths. You'll be given the opportunity to examine other fact witnesses when the issue of the bill is resolved. As you know, examinations are held in the courthouse, so check with the official reporter for a date. Expert witnesses will be examined after both sides have finished with the other parties. Who's your expert?"

"I don't know yet, Your Honor. We're looking for one now."

"When each of you has your expert, you will give written notice to your adversary of his or her name, address, and qualifications."

We both nodded.

"And whom will you be examining, Mr. Bennett? I assume the proponent, the witnesses, and the scrivener?"

"It's not an attorney-drawn will, Your Honor," I pointed out. "The decedent dictated his own will."

"I do want to examine one additional person, Your Honor," said Bennett.

"Who's that?" asked the judge.

"Mr. Elkins."

". . . Whatever for?"

"He's the one who forged the will."

"That's utter *nonsense*!" I shouted.

The judge held up his hand. "That is an extremely serious accusation. Do you really have evidence on that?"

"I'll have some by the time of trial."

"You'd better." The judge turned and considered me thoughtfully. He was about to say something but changed his mind and looked back at Bennett. "I'll hold your request to examine Mr. Elkins in abeyance. First we'll have the examinations of all the other fact witnesses. Then ask for another conference, and we'll see."

"But Your Honor, I'm entitled—"

The judge held up his hand. "You've heard my decision." He remained still for a moment. Then he took another sip of coffee and looked down at some notes he had been making. "I assume that, under the circumstances, neither of you wants to talk settlement."

"Settlement discussions are always appropriate, Your Honor," I replied, knowing that's what a judge wanted to hear.

"I don't discuss settlement with forgers," said Bennett.

"So be it," replied the judge. "Notice your examinations, and, Mr. Bennett, you have one week to respond to the bill of particulars demand. Please ask the clerk to call the next conference."

ON THE FOLLOWING WEDNESDAY, on my return to the office from Landlord and Tenant, I picked up a phone message from my former boss, Bill Anderson. I returned the call and got Anderson's voice mail. Later that afternoon my intercom buzzed.

"Yes, Rosie."

"Mr. Anderson's on the line."

"Hi, Bill. How're you doing?"

"Just fine, Ian, and you?"

"Great, what's up?"

"Can you come in and see me some time tomorrow?"

"How about lunch? It's been too long?"

"No. This isn't a social call."

". . .Is there something wrong?"

"I don't want to discuss it over the phone. When can you come in?"

"I'm in Landlord and Tenant tomorrow morning. I'll stop in as soon as I'm finished."

"I'll see you then. If it's later than one, please call me."

At 1:00 THE NEXT DAY, I STILL had two more cases in Landlord and Tenant. I stepped out of the courtroom and called. "I'm running late."

"When *can* you make it?"

"I should be done here by two."

"Stop in at three."

"See you."

I called Herb Crowley to see if he could join me for a late lunch, but Herb had already left for lunch. So after eating alone, I appeared at Anderson's office promptly at three. There was little or no change in the principal attorney's room since I had worked for him. The ancient rectangular wooden desk was loaded with files. The two windows behind the desk were, as usual, translucent with dirt. The tall, angular chief was seated behind his desk, his heels resting on the chair to his left, his writing pullout loaded with papers, talking on the phone. I picked up the pile of files from the least loaded of the visitor's chairs and sat down.

Five minutes later, Anderson hung up the phone. "Hi, Ian."

"Hi, yourself. What's the big mystery?"

"No mystery. The boss had a disturbing conversation about you and asked me to call you in."

"From whom, and about what?"

"Coffee first."

I rose, went to the coffee maker on the stand near the door, poured two cups, added sugar and creamer to Bill's, passed it over and resumed my seat. The routine brought back fond memories. When I was with the court, only the judge, chief clerk, and chief law assistant had their own coffee makers. When I wanted coffee, I'd visit Bill's office on the pretext of discussing a case.

We sipped. I decided not to push. Finally after five minutes of sipping and staring, Bill spoke up. "The boss goes to meetings of the local surrogate's association quite regularly."

"I hear he's the vice president," I replied with a nod.

"There was a meeting Monday night."

I remained silent.

"As you know, the boss has been spreading your name around to his colleagues. Recommending you for guardianship appointments."

"That's very kind of him. Tell him thanks."

"On Monday night, Al Carter, from Westchester buttonholed him." Anderson looked down at a yellow legal pad on the pull out. "He mentioned a McGrath estate?"

"That's mine. I was before him last Friday."

"He told the boss you've been accused of forging the will."

"Yup."

"You didn't, did you?" Anderson said with a shocked expression.

"Of course not. I don't know if there was a forgery, but I sure didn't do it."

"The boss didn't think so. Neither did I." Anderson's expression displayed relief. "What's it about?"

"Remember Joe Bennett?"

Anderson thought a moment. "Didn't he do Iron Curtain kinship cases? He was in the same office as Taylor?"

I nodded.

"He's on the other side?"

I nodded again.

"It figures. Have you checked the will with your handwriting expert?"

"Not yet—the client insisted on picking her own. I was just given the name. Mario Gambi. Do you know him?"

"Heard of him," Anderson replied, frowning.

". . .And?"

"Lousy reputation."

"Does Judge Carter really believe I forged a will?"

Anderson hesitated and took a swig of his coffee. "No, but you know, where there's smoke . . ."

CHAPTER SEVEN

HE OFFICES OF MCGRATH RESIDENTIALS occupied a ground floor apartment of one of their buildings in the West Bronx. At 4:30 on Thursday afternoon Alice entered the office after completing her rounds. The one-bedroom apartment laid out very well for an office: the living room-dining area had been converted into a reception area and secretarial room. The kitchen served as the lunchroom, and contained her photo copier and fax. The bedroom was the executive office. Elena Rodriguez, a trim Hispanic woman who doubled as a receptionist and secretary said hello. "Gee, am I glad you stopped in, Alice. The phone's been ringing off the hook."

"Yeah? What's up?"

"Manny's been calling. You got ten cases on in Brooklyn tomorrow. He wants to meet you for breakfast before court."

"Call him and tell him I'll be at Cookies at 8:15. What else?"

"The super at 127th Street's been calling. They're having a rent strike."

"Call Mr. Cohen. Tell him to start dispossess. We'll work something out in court. What else?"

"We got four calls from some woman from Texas—says she's a nun."

"Oh, shit—my Holy Roller fucking cousin. What does she want?"

"She didn't say. She wants you to call her," Elena concluded with a disapproving look. She didn't like that kind of a reference to a nun.

"Give me her number. I'll call her from home tonight. What else?"

Elena shook her head.

"Give me the mail."

Elena complied, and Alice retired to her office to read. By 5:15 she'd finished and left for home. She parked her BMW in a garage on Boston Road. It was a five-block walk to her apartment, but she wasn't going to leave a Beemer on the street in that neighborhood. Uncle Jim had bought it for her—the only expensive present he'd ever given her. She'd wondered at the time whether it was an advance payment for sex, but he'd never tried.

At home she made a double Black Label on the rocks and sipped it slowly. She was about to start dinner when she remembered Mary Elizabeth and picked up the phone. It warbled, telling her there were messages on her voice mail. She checked. One was from Manny Romero, the lawyer she used for her Brooklyn cases, confirming break-fast at Cookies. Three of the others were from Mary Eliz-abeth. God, her cousin was a pain in the ass. She phoned the convent and was told Sister was at prayer. She would call her back later. Alice shrugged, tossed off the balance of her drink, made a refill and put some chops in a pan. By eight-thirty, she'd just finished dinner, put her dishes and the pan into the sink, and was pouring herself a Grand Marnier when the phone rang. "Hello?"

"Alice?"

"Hi, Mary Elizabeth, how are you?" Alice asked, taking a sip of the sweet liqueur.

"Well, thank God. And you?"

"Everything's just peachy. What's up?"

"You remember our discussion at Uncle Jim's wake?"

"Not really," Alice lied.

"I was telling you about the problems of our order and how repairs to the convent were crucial."

"Yeah, you said something like that."

"And I told you that Uncle Jim had assured mother and

me that he'd made provision for us in his will. As a matter of fact he said he'd left nearly everything to us."

"You did say something like that, and I told you that his will left everything to Moira and me."

"What about the lawyer-drawn will you told me about?"

"Mary Elizabeth, all I said to you was that he had mentioned he once had a lawyer draw a will. He never showed it to me, and he didn't tell me who the lawyer was. I know it wasn't any of the ones who represent the business. But, even if he *had* had one, he must have changed his mind."

"Uncle Jim would never have done that. He made a promise to the church. His immortal soul is in jeopardy."

Alice had a difficult time controlling an urge to laugh. "Look, Mary Elizabeth, I don't think Uncle Jim will go to hell because he left his money to his favorite nieces, but I'll tell you what—when the will is probated, I'll consider giving something to your order."

"How much? The repairs we need will cost millions."

"Grow up, cousin. That's not in the cards."

"Then we will have to fight for our rights. Mother will be in touch with our lawyer."

"Do what you want," Alice replied, and hung up.

ON SATURDAY WE GOT HOME a little before midnight from an evening with the Crowleys and went straight to bed.

Feeling romantic, I began to caress my wife, but when I went beyond stroking her back she pushed me off. "Sorry, sweetie, but I'm very tired. I need my beauty sleep."

"Okay," I half groaned. "I'll see you in the morning."

We slept till 9:00. When I awoke, I was still in the mood for love. I reached for her and was again rebuffed. "Hey, what's the matter. Are you mad at me or something?"

"No, it's just. . .my stomach feels queasy."

She rose and repaired to the bathroom. When she returned, I noticed that her breath smelled of mouthwash. "You okay?" I asked.

"A little better. I had to throw up."

"Your stomach's been bothering you for the last few weeks. Maybe you should see a doctor."

"I have an appointment for Wednesday after work, but I think I know what she'll tell me."

"What?"

"Remember when we went away to Spring Lake?"

"Sure. Great weekend. The sex was fabulous—at least for me."

"It was, for me too, but I forgot to pack my diaphragm, and with the rain on Saturday night I didn't want to send you chasing around for a drug store."

"You think. . . ?"

She nodded.

"That's earlier than we'd planned."

She nodded again.

"It sort of puts a hole in our finances."

"So what do you want to do?" she asked, her expression turning grave.

I thought for a moment. "Hey, that's your decision, not mine. I mean, it's your body."

"And what if it *were* your decision?"

"I may be old-fashioned, but that's our baby."

She smiled as she hugged me. Then her expression turned serious. "I'm sure Mom and Dad would help out."

"No way. This is *my* family."

She shook her head. She believed we could have been married a lot sooner if I weren't so stubborn and had accepted the family help, but she told me that was one of the reasons she loved me.

". . .I just thought of something."

"What?"

"The real problem's the medical."

"You're covered by medical insurance at the office. Your firm's plan is a lot better than Mark's. It should cover the maternity."

"Sure—and then what? What if I can't go back to work at the end of my maternity leave? What do we do for medical then?"

"What's your idea?"

"When you were with the court, you had a *great* medical plan."

"So?"

"So why don't you ask the judge to take you back?"

". . .That's not so easy. In the first place, there may not be any openings now."

"So ask for the next one that comes up."

"And they may not want me back."

"Why?"

I told her about my meeting with Bill Anderson.

"I guess," she agreed, "you're going to have to get through McGrath first."

"YOU'RE A VERY POPULAR MAN, MR. ELKINS," Rosemary Lennon announced as I entered the office after court that Monday.

"You mean you just found out?" I looked into my box and extracted a small stack of phone slips. "Who called, Miss America?"

"You're not *that* popular. Mr. McGrath."

"James McGrath? Back from the grave?"

"No, Charles. Three times."

"I wonder what *he* wants. Doesn't he know he's supposed to contact me through his lawyer?"

The phone rang. ". . . .One moment, sir. I'll put him on." Rosie looked back up. "It's him."

I grabbed my mail and messages, hung up my coat, and picked up the phone in my office. "Hello, Mr. McGrath—

what can I do for you?"

"You see, Mr. Elkins, it's this case. I don't like what's going on."

"Does your lawyer know you're calling me?"

"What lawyer?"

"Mr. Bennett."

"No, he's my *brother's* lawyer."

"Then why did you sign the power of attorney appointing him as *your* lawyer? It's on file in the clerk's office."

"My brother said I had to—otherwise, Alice would steal Jim's estate."

"Then why are you calling me? As long as Joe Bennett is your official attorney, I'm not supposed to talk to you about the case."

"I don't want to see Alice hurt."

"So withdraw from the case and join her."

"Then I won't get anything."

"Are you trying to tell me that you want to make a settlement?"

"Yeah, I guess so."

"There are only two ways you can do that."

"What?"

"You can fire Joe Bennett. Then I can talk to you."

"If I do that and we *don't* settle, then I won't have a lawyer."

"That's true, but there's another way. Talk to Alice."

TWO NIGHTS LATER, ALICE KELLER answered a buzz on the intercom. "Yeah?"

"It's me, your uncle Charlie."

"My lawyer said you might be calling. Come on in." She pressed the buzzer and, a minute later, he entered.

"Good seeing you, Alice," he said, reaching to kiss her.

She avoided his grasp. A three-day growth of beard did not invite even a filial kiss, and he exuded an aroma that evidenced a lack of bathing for even longer. "Take off your coat and have a seat in the living room."

As he removed his lined raincoat, she observed that he was attired in a not-too-clean white work uniform, and hoped nothing would come off on her furniture. "It smells good," he said.

"It's pork chops. I just finished dinner. I've got some coffee up. You want some?"

"Got anything stronger?" he asked as he seated himself on the couch.

"Wine, beer, scotch, or Irish?" she asked. Noticing that he seemed to be leering at her, she pulled her blue terry cloth robe close and tightened the tie.

"Irish on the rocks would be great."

She went to the kitchen and returned a few minutes later with a mug of coffee and a bowl of ice. She laid the coffee on a cocktail table and took the ice to the bar, where she put three cubes in a roly-poly glass, filled it with Jameson's, put it on the table in front of him, picked up her coffee, and seated herself on an easy chair.

They sipped for the next five minutes. He looked up at the wall behind her to stare at an oil painting of a nude leaning against a tree. She must be doing good, he thought. Finally he broke the silence. "You're looking okay, Alice."

"Thanks, but I sure you didn't come all this way just to tell me that."

He giggled. "Well, your lawyer must have told you why I've come."

"Yeah, he said you wanted to settle. What've you got in mind?"

"Well, look, you know I like—I mean, love—you."

She shrugged.

"And I don't want to see Hal hurt you."

She looked at him.

"So if you just drop the probate of that phony will, we can all split the estate and all go home happy."

". . .Are you out of your fucking gourd?"

He sat dumbfounded for a moment. "What if I dropped my opposition to the will?"

"And?"

"You could probate the will, and we would split fifty-fifty."

She looked at him.

"What's wrong with that?"

"For one thing, what about Uncle Hal?"

"He'd be alone. We'd beat him."

"Grow up, Charlie. I told you what I'd do if you consented to the will."

"What was that?"

"What's the matter, your short term memory slipping? I said that, when the will was probated, I'd give you a job with the real estate company and something extra."

"How much?"

"I'll decide then."

"And what about now? I need money now."

"I won't *have* it till then."

"So I guess we'll have to whip your ass."

"You can try. For now, get the hell out of here." She rose and turned towards the door.

Charlie came after her and reached out. She stepped back, but he'd caught her robe and pulled it open, revealing her naked except for a pair of skin tight panties. He grinned and reached for her left breast. She backed towards the kitchen, and he followed. When he reached out with both arms to embrace her, she stepped in and kneed him in the groin. He bent forward; she brought her knee up into his face. He stood still in shock, and his nose began to bleed. She removed his coat from the hall closet, grabbed a handful of his hair and dragged him through the doorway, down the hall, out the front door, and pushed him down the stoop. Then she threw his coat on top of him and returned to the apartment.

CHAPTER EIGHT

T WAS DARK BY THE TIME I drove my Volvo to the East Bronx. I was not in the best of moods: As clients went, Alice Keller was a pain in the ass. Client meetings were supposed to take place at the lawyer's office and generally during normal business hours. The only place I had ever met Alice was at her apartment, and then usually in the evening. I'd tried to insist that she conform to normal practice, to no avail. She was quite straightforward about it—no resort to feminine wiles. "Look, Ian," she said. "I work long hours running McGrath. I can't spare a half day to come to your office, and in the evening I'm too damned tired to go out."

The meeting was absolutely crucial. Bennett and I had

scheduled her deposition and the other two witnesses for the following morning, and I hadn't even met the latter, much less prepared them. So I parked my car and walked the two blocks to Alice's building. The three teenage boys were, as usual, stationed in front, but by then they knew me well enough to greet me rather than play building security.

Alice opened the apartment door and ushered me into the living room, where she and the witnesses were having an after-dinner drink. All three were in jeans and white golf shirts without logos, but there the similarity ended. Lester Smith and Alice were seated together on a love seat facing the couch. He was clean shaven except for his mustache. His muscular arms and shoulders tapered to a slim waist and hips. Jack Gorman took up over half of the long couch. The bushy black beard that covered most of his face was in bad need of a trimming, and a monumental stomach obscured his lap.

After being introduced and shaking hands, I accepted a cup of coffee, seated myself on an armchair, and took out a yellow legal pad. I explained that they were going to be examined under oath by Hal McGrath's lawyer at the courthouse the next day. I asked about their relationship to the parties. Gorman had known Moira for three years before her death from cancer and had become engaged to her a year before she died—six months after Jim McGrath signed the will. Lester Smith had been dating Alice for a year before the will was signed. Each had had a cordial relation-ship with the deceased. Both worked in the back office of a brokerage firm, and Jack had introduced Les to Alice. They each gave the same account of the will preparation and signing that Alice had. I gave them a few rules on how to conduct themselves, including a final admonition to tell only the absolute truth.

After I left, Jack asked Alice, "Where'd you find *that* boy scout?"

She laughed. "He is sort of like one, but he's a good wills lawyer, he knows what he's doing, and, best of all, he looks honest."

They all laughed. "Well," Les remarked, "*we're* not."

"What's that supposed to mean?" she demanded.

"What it sounds like," said Jack. "Boy scouts do good deeds for free."

"So?"

"So what's in it for us if we support your story?"

"You heard what I told you," she replied. "You split a mil if the will goes through."

"No way, Alice," said Les. "We've been thinking."

"About what?"

"Less than ten percent of the estate is kind of chintzy for what we're doing for you."

She frowned. "What do you think you're worth?"

"At least two mil, and that's a bargain," Les replied with

a smile.

". . .That's extortion."

Les shrugged.

"Take it or leave it, Alice," Jack added. "You sign on the dotted line now," he said, proffering a set of papers.

"Or?" she asked, crestfallen.

"Or tomorrow we do what your lawyer told us to do," Les said with a smirk. "We tell the absolute truth."

THE DEPOSITION WAS BEING HELD at 9:30 a.m. in a window-less ten-by-fifteen room. My clients were half an hour late. The reporter, a slightly overweight blonde in a jean skirt and leather-fringed jean top, was seated next to her machine at the near end of an eight-foot table, with Bennett and Hal along the back side. "So you got here," Bennett griped. "It's about time."

I ignored him and gave the reporter my card.

"I'll start with him," Bennett snapped, pointing to Jack. "You two wait outside."

"Les, please wait outside," I said.

"What about her?"

"My client's a party, and she'll stay."

Bennett snorted.

Jack and Les testified exactly as they had told it to me the night before. Bennett brought out their relationship to Alice and Moira as well as their desire for Alice to get the estate, all of which they freely admitted, but, on the whole, their depositions were uneventful. At one point in Les's testimony, Bennett wanted to know how much he was being paid to lie. He blandly replied, "Well, she bought me a good breakfast this morning, but I'm not being paid, and I'm telling the truth just like the lawyer told me."

Les's examination ended at a quarter to one, and at Hal's insistence, we broke for lunch. The opposing sides ate at opposing ends of a coffee shop two blocks from the courthouse, They ordered the same things, too. For me, Alice, Les, and Bennett, it was bison burgers and coffee; Hal, Charlie, and Jack gorged on double cheeseburgers and chocolate shakes.

The depositions resumed at two. For the first hour Bennett's examination of Alice was not combative. He asked about her family, her deceased sister, and their relationship with James McGrath. Then he went into her employment by her uncle. After what seemed ages, he took her step by step through the will signing. By the time he had finished, he could have hosted a birthday party just like Moira's. Finally, he stopped asking questions, studied his notes, and had a whispered conversation with Hal, after which he returned to notes.

After nearly ten minutes of inaction, I asked, "Are you finished?"

"Far from it. I just want to be sure I've covered the

mundane—but now we'll get to the good part."

I shrugged, and Bennett went back to his papers. After another five minutes he lifted his head and fixed Alice with a stare. "So tell me, Ms. Keller, where did you forge your uncle's will?"

"I didn't forge anything."

"Was it at the birthday party, or was it too busy then with your uncle looking on?"

"I told you, I didn't forge it," she replied, her face reddening.

Hal snickered.

"If you didn't do it, who did? Was it your boyfriend?"

"No."

"Your sister's boyfriend?"

"No."

"Then who was it? Don't keep me in suspense. Was it your shyster lawyer?"

"*Objection!*" I shouted.

"What's the matter, counselor, are you afraid of the truth?"

"Objection, objection, objection. Why don't you ask proper questions and stop badgering the witness?"

"Yes, you shouldn't accuse Mr. Elkins of that. He's an honorable lawyer."

"How would you know that?"

"I can tell. He's been my family's lawyer for a long

time."

"You mean he represented your uncle, too?"

"No, just my sister and me."

"For how long?"

"Quite a while."

"And that's why you hired him for this case, because he's a good forger?"

"That will be quite enough," I said, seething. "Let's go." Alice and I rose and turned to the door.

"How *dare* you walk out of an examination?" Bennett demanded.

"If you knew how to *conduct* one, we wouldn't have to, but I will not allow you to subject my client to abuse. If you want a further examination, the judge will have to order it," I concluded, and turned to Alice. "Meet me downstairs in the lobby." When she left the room, I turned to the reporter. "I'll be back in a few minutes to start the examinations of the objectants."

"Like hell you will," Bennett replied.

"What do you mean by that?"

"You'll get your examination of my clients when I've finished with yours."

"You've finished with my client."

"When the judge says I have." Bennett motioned, and the three rose.

"For the record, Mr. Bennett, your clients are noticed

for examination today."

"They will be here when the court orders them, and not before," Bennett said as they marched through the doorway.

Alice was waiting when I came down. "What the hell did you mean that I'd been your family's lawyer for a long time?"

"Well, this case has been going on for a long time," she replied, looking flustered.

"I never *met* your sister. How could I have represented her?"

"Uncle Jim's will left everything to Moira and me, so I always think of your representing both of us. Will it do any harm?"

"It sure could."

"Then why did we just walk out? Why didn't you do something about it?"

"I didn't want to ask you any questions about that. I didn't know what you would say. We'll explain it in an affidavit when you sign your deposition, and hope it doesn't hurt too much."

I left the courthouse with a queasy feeling in my stomach.

ALGERNON FLYNN WAS A HANDSOME young man of nearly thirty, six-feet two and slim, with straight black hair. He played tournament squash. From a wealthy Catholic family in Boston, he had received an extensive education in schools affiliated with the Church.   After graduating high in his class from Georgetown Law, he secured employment with Duffy, Donovan, and Sala, a small, prestigious New York City law firm with luxurious offices in Rockefeller Center. Over the years, several of the partners had had strong connections with the Church, and Jerry Donovan, Jr., the managing partner, was a boyhood friend of the cardinal. For those reasons, the firm had earned a nice piece of the Archdiocese's business, including substantial estates.

One Tuesday morning, Flynn was sipping coffee and reading the *Law Journal* in his nine-by-twelve interior office when he was called into the managing partner's eighteen-by-twenty-three foot windowed chambers.

"Good morning, sir. Isn't it a lovely day?" he asked as he entered.

Donovan nodded, rose from behind his pin-neat oval desk, and turned toward the conversation area to the left of the door. "Sit down, Algernon," he said, motioning the other to the love seat against the wall. He seated himself in a tan leather armchair on the opposite side of a glass-topped cocktail table.

Algernon complied but said nothing further, maintaining a broad smile to hide his nervousness. He worked for the estates partner and had had little contact with this man. Since he had been with the firm for nearly six years, they were supposed to tell him whether he was being seriously considered for partnership or was on a downward slide. Donovan generally delivered that kind of news.

The older man did not speak for several minutes as he fingered his bristly black mustache. Algernon's eyes were fixed on a belly that protruded from a blue-striped, unbuttoned vest.

"Algernon," Donovan finally said, "Matt Bowen has spoken highly of you. He likes your work, and he thinks you have considerable tact and discretion."

"I'm glad to know that, sir," Flynn replied with a feeling of relief. "It's been a pleasure working for Mr. Bowen."

"Cardinal Regan has asked us to handle a small matter that will require both tact and discretion, and Matt thinks you're the one for the job." Donovan picked up a thin file from the table and placed it on his lap. "He's received a request for help from the archbishop in Houston. It seems that one of his convents has been promised a large bequest from the uncle of one of the sisters. The uncle's will is being probated in Westchester County. It makes no provision for the convent. I've ordered a copy of the probate file. It appears that everything has been left to a niece. The other relatives are objecting to probate on the grounds of forgery, but even if probate is denied the convent stands to get very little or nothing, and the sisters need the money to make repairs. Look into it and see whether you can finesse something so that they continue to have a roof over their heads."

A FEW DAYS LATER, I RECEIVED A CALL from Flynn, who explained that he was representing the Convent of the Sacred Heart and believed that we could help each other. We agreed to meet, though Flynn insisted it be at his office, where he knew he would impress the yokel from the Bronx. The next afternoon I emerged from the elevator at 650 Avenue of the Americas directly into the reception area of Duffy, Donovan and Sala. The pretty young receptionist with the slightly upturned nose and a mild brogue told me that Mr. Flynn was expecting me. She asked me to have a seat, took my coat, and hung it in a wardrobe.

While I waited, I looked around. The walls were decorated with art that looked, at least to my untrained eye, like original oils. A few minutes later, a curly-haired blonde with a truly voluptuous figure, also sporting a faint brogue, escorted me to a conference room. The continuous-grain redwood paneling of the twenty-by-twelve foot room was also hung with oil paintings, several of barristers in robes and wigs. "Mr. Flynn will be with you shortly," she said. "May I get you some coffee?"

I assented, and she served me in a delicate white-and-blue china cup together with a plate of butter cookies. I seated myself at the fourteen-foot, glass-topped conference table and waited for my host.

"I'm sorry to have kept you," Flynn announced when he arrived twenty minutes later. "The phone hasn't stopped ringing."

"Fear not—the meter's running, and I'll bill you."

We both laughed, and shook hands. Flynn helped himself to coffee, then joined me at the conference table. His attire oozed wealth and power; the medium blue herringbone suit, either Brooks Brothers or J. Press, fit him to perfection. His pale blue oxford shirt sported a tie decorated with squash racquet designs that didn't come from a street vendor's cart.

After a few minutes of pleasantries, he got down to business. "As I told you over the phone, the archdiocese is very interested in the McGrath estate. There are four family members who take in the absence of a will, one of whom is Mary Curran, James's sister. Her daughter, Mary Elizabeth, is a teaching sister at the Sacred Heart Convent in Houston. James made numerous promises to leave all or most of his estate to the order, which is in desperate need of money to make repairs to the convent. They are morally certain that there's a lawyer-drawn will with those provisions, and they believe that your will must be a forgery."

I sighed. "Mr. Flynn, while I'm personally in favor of helping worthy charities, we're obviously on opposing sides, and I can't see how we can help each other."

"*Au contraire*, Ian—may I call you that?"

I nodded.

"And please call me Algernon. We are *definitely* in a position to help each other."

I was puzzled.

"Think of it this way," he said. "If we can't work something out and I join the opposition, I think the power of the church wouldn't do your case any good, but what would it get me? Very little. Mrs. Curran's share would only be a quarter, and even if she were willing to give it all to the convent, her daughter would insist that she keep most of it for herself, which won't help the convent until she dies. Assuming your client *loses* the probate, her share gets cut down from all to a quarter, and I think there's at least a fair chance that we'll be able to find the real will, which either leaves it all to the convent or part to it and some to your client."

"So?" I asked impatiently.

"So we join forces. I'll either find the true will or help you get your will probated."

"And what do you get out of it?"

"As I see it, each of us runs a risk. It your will is probated, we get nothing, and if ours is, you come up empty. I suggest we agree to cut our losses. If you prevail, give us a third, and we'll do the same if ours is probated."

"What if neither is probated?"

"Your lady keeps her quarter of the estate. That way, no matter what happens, she gets something."

I sat in silence for several minutes. Flynn finally said, "Well, what do you think?"

"Very interesting. I'll talk to my client."

A few minutes after I left, Flynn was summoned into the managing partner's office. "Well, how did you do?" Donovan asked.

Algernon explained.

"Good thinking, my boy. Keep at it. If you can work this one out, you'll have a good future with the firm."

Algernon left his chambers with a reflective smile on his lips.

CHAPTER NINE

T WAS 6:30 IN THE EVENING when Mary Curran pulled her green Mustang into the driveway. The forty-five-minute trek from her bookkeeping job in a hospital in downtown Houston to her two-bedroom townhouse in the suburbs had exhausted her. It'd been a hot day, and the air conditioner was barely working. When her husband died five years before, she'd been very fortunate that the life insurance had paid off the car loan, but the vehicle was really getting old—just like her.

She parked it in the garage and entered the house. It was much cooler there; she began to feel better. After washing her face, she went into the kitchen to fix a vodka and tonic. But as she approached the refrigerator, she noticed the flashing light on the answering machine—a message from her brother.

Good old Hal had been a godsend since John died. He'd reorganized her finances and invested for her. She'd done quite well. The income was adequate for her needs, and the investments had outperformed the Dow. Even better, he'd charged her only a nominal fee—a lot less than she'd have had to pay an investment advisor.

She settled down on the recliner in the minuscule second bedroom that served as a family room, took the first sip of her drink—and did it taste good—before picking up the portable phone.

"Hi, Carol, it's Mary. How are you?"

"Okay, I guess."

"What's the matter?"

"Oh, nothing, I'm fine," Carol replied in a shaky voice.

"You sure? You sound terrible—real down."

"I'm okay. It's just . . . ."

"What is it? Hal?" Mary was becoming concerned.

"Sort of."

"Has he been slapping you around again?" Mary demanded.

"No, it's not that. He's been drinking more and not watching his diet. He's gotten so fat."

"Do you want me to talk to him about it?"

"No, I'll handle it. What's up with you?"

"I'm fine. Is he in? He left a message for me to call him."

"No, he's at Sculley's, knocking back a few with his buddies. I'll have him call you when he staggers in."

Mary had her dinner, watched the news on television, and was preparing for bed when the phone rang.

"Hal?"

"Who the hell d'ja think it was?"

She bit back a sarcastic retort. "I'm sorry. How are you?"

"Why should you care?"

"*Please*, Hal. What's the matter? Of course I care."

"Then why are you doing this to me?"

". . .Doing what?"

"As if you didn't know. Opposing me over Jim's estate."

"I'm *not* doing that. I haven't done anything at *all*."

"That's bad enough. You're sitting on your hands while Charlie and I have to fight a phony will."

"You know I can't afford a lawyer. Besides, you never *asked* me to join you."

"Don't hand me that crap. What about your daughter?"

"What *about* Mary Elizabeth?"

"Don't tell me you didn't know."

"She *did* mention something about Jim's promise to the convent. He did *promise*, you know."

"Yeah, you and that goddamn church of yours pushed him into saying something, but Jim was too smart to do anything that stupid."

"Hal, it's your church, too. Mom and Dad brought us up right."

"A lot good that did me."

Again she bit her tongue.

"Now, you listen good. Have that daughter of yours mind her business and get out of the case, and you come in with us. I'll pick up your advance legals. You can pay it back from your share of Jim's estate."

"Hal, I'm not *involved* with Mary Elizabeth. It's the *convent* that's doing it."

"Cow shit! Let me make myself clear. Either you get Mary Elizabeth and that fucking convent to back down, or you're going to be one poor woman."

"But my investments are doing fine. . . you *wouldn't*!"

"Wouldn't I?" he replied, breaking the connection.

AT ABOUT THAT TIME, I WAS TRYING to arrange a meeting with Alice to discuss Algernon Flynn's offer. I'd made several calls to both her apartment and office, but none had been returned. Finally, one evening at ten-fifteen, after Helen and I returned from dinner at a local restaurant, I called the apartment and got an answer.

"Alice?"

"Yeah, who's this?"

"Ian."

"Why are you calling this late?"

"I've called you a half a dozen times and left messages," I snapped back.

". . .I've been kind of busy. What's up?"

Probably screwing the neighborhood, I thought. Grow up and stop being so judgmental, my other self added. "It's the case."

"Obviously."

"Why so glum?" Helen asked when I hung up the phone. "Alice?"

My mood brightened as I examined her. She looked really great. The pregnancy had added radiance to her face but didn't yet show on her slim body, the morning sickness had abated, and our sex life had resumed. "Who else?"

"What'd she want?"

"For me to come over to her apartment now."

"At this hour? What is she, nuts or oversexed?"

"Probably both."

"So what are you going to do?"

"I'll see her tomorrow night at six."

"Haven't you forgotten something?" Helen asked, her face hardening.

"I know, tomorrow is Friday and we're due at your folks for dinner. I'll have to grab a sandwich before the meeting and pick you up after I'm through." I knew Molly would be hurt, but Sam would understand.

MOLLY HAD MADE ROAST CHICKEN with honeyed carrots, and baked potatoes, chicken soup with matzo balls, and a green salad. At the dining room table sat the usual complement—Betty and Eric Goldstein, their two children, Sam, Molly, and Helen. There was an empty place setting for me. Betty and Helen were clearing the main course from the table as Molly brought in a large apple pie and a dish of vanilla ice cream.

"Where's the lawyer who makes house calls?" Sam asked.

As if in answer to his question, the bell rang. Freddy Goldstein sprung from his seat and rushed to the door. "Uncle Ian's here!" he shouted.

I picked him up, kissed him, carried him to the dining room, and deposited him on his seat, after which I kissed my niece and each of the women.

"Sit down, Ian. I'll get you some dinner. You must be starved."

"No, thanks, Mom. I ate before my meeting."

"At least have some of this delicious pie and ice cream."

"Just give him a sliver of pie and a dab of ice cream, Mom," Helen cut in as I was nodding assent.

"Oh, come on, Helen. He works hard and needs his

nourishment."

"*Please*, Mom, don't encourage him. He's getting too fat."

Molly compromised by giving me a medium sized slice, half of what she had intended. After dessert the children went to Sam's den to play while we all repaired to the living room for coffee.

"Tell us about the house call," Sam said.

I described my meeting with Algernon Flynn.

"Sounds like a fair offer. What did the lady say?"

"Not much. I told her I thought it was a good deal. She said she'd think it over and let me know in a few days."

JACK GORMAN'S STOMACH JIGGLED in rhythm with his laughter. "You must be pulling my leg, Alice." It was Saturday afternoon, and the three were sitting in Alice's living room, drinking Black Bush.

She took a gulp of her drink, slammed the glass down on the cocktail table only half on its coaster, and wiped up the spill with a tissue. "What the hell is so funny?"

"That should be obvious," Lester replied, and took a sip of his Irish. He wasn't laughing.

She glared at him. "It's not obvious to me. I tell you about a sensible business proposition that my lawyer recommends to me, and instead of a sensible response, this fat idiot laughs up a storm and you tell me it's funny. I don't get it."

Lester shook his head. "Look, Alice, we can't believe you're that stupid. You must be putting us on." He frowned, "In any case it's your stupid idea. Why'd you call us in?"

"If I only get two-thirds and still have all the expense and taxes, I can't afford to pay you the two million. We're going to have to change the deal."

Jack turned toward Les, pointed to Alice, then to the side of his head, and made circles with his finger.

Les nodded.

"What the fuck is that?" Alice shouted.

"I thought that was obvious, too. Where I went to school that always meant that you're nuts."

She squeezed the arm of her chair and brought herself under control. "Look, there's a serious problem, and I've got a solution that will help all of us. At least listen!"

Les rose, picked up the bottle, topped off the drinks, and resumed his seat. "She's buying. Tell us."

She cleared her throat. "As I see it, if the convent finds a will leaving everything to them, we're out. I've heard Uncle Jim talk about Mary Elizabeth's convent, and I'm pretty sure he wanted to do something for them."

"So?" Jack asked.

"So there's a fair chance they'll find that will, and this deal is insurance for all of us. If our will goes through, I get two-thirds and you two split a mil and a third. If the convent's will succeeds, I get a third and you two split two thirds of a mil. It seems fair to me."

Les smiled and shook his head. "I'll tell you how we see it. It your will goes through, you get two-thirds and we get two mil, and if the convent's will makes it, you get a third and we get two mil."

"Yeah," said Jack, wiping his face on his sleeve. "You tell us some fancy lawyer told your lawyer you should give a third of Jim's estate to a convent in Texas, and you expect us to contribute to it? You must think we're nuts."

"It makes sense to me. This way at least we all get something. If we lose this case, I get a lousy quarter, and I *could* have to pay everybody's legals out of it."

Lester shook his head and began in a tone one uses to an errant child, "Alice, I think you need a lesson in the facts of life, and I guess Uncle Les will have to give it to you. Your uncle's will leaves everything to you. When the will is probated, you pay Jack and me two million for our services and keep the rest. If we lose, you get a quarter."

"So?" she asked, nodding.

"So if you give away a third of the estate, on the un-likely chance that Jim had a will leaving everything to this convent, you can't possibly think we're going to contribute to your stupidity."

Alice sat glumly for a few minutes. Suddenly, her face

brightened. "Well, that's what I'm going to do. If you don't like it, sue me. My lawyer will defend me, and you won't get a dime."

"And what if we decide to tell the truth when the case goes to court?" Jack asked with a smile.

"You already testified a few weeks ago. If you change your story at trial, you'll go to jail for perjury."

Les smiled. "Then I guess the three of us will have adjoining cells."

CHAPTER
TEN

A FEW WEEKS LATER, I FOUND AN ENVELOPE in my in-basket with Bennett's return address and transcripts of the depositions of Alice and the two witnesses, together with a letter giving me detailed instructions that they were to be executed before a notary public and returned. It cited a court rule that prohibited me from making any physical changes or corrections to the transcript except by affidavit. The envelope also contained a copy of a letter from Bennett to Judge Carter, stating that Alice and I had walked out of her deposition before it was concluded, that I was involved in the forgery, and that, "rather than bother the court with an unnecessary motion, a conference be scheduled so that Ms. Keller be ordered to appear for the resumption of her deposition, and that Mr. Elkins be directed to appear for his deposition."

I immediately began to draft a response. By the next day, after going through four drafts, I was ready to send it out. Just as I was about to sign the letter, my intercom buzzed.

"Mr. Elkins, you have a call on ten."

"Who from?"

"Mr. McCullough, from the surrogate's court."

I answered it.

"Hi. I'm Frank McCullough, Judge Carter's law secretary. He's gotten a letter from your adversary, Mr. Bennett, in the McGrath Estate."

"I know. I was just about to send the judge my response."

"Don't bother. We assume you disagree."

"Yup."

"The judge wants to hold a conference. How's this Friday at two?"

I looked at my diary. "I can make it. Can Bennett?"

"Yes. I just got off the phone with him."

"Where's it going to be, it the courtroom?"

"No, in chambers."

THAT FRIDAY AT 1:00, I PARKED In the White Plains municipal garage. I had my lunch at the local bagel shop—remembering my dietary vow, a seafood salad on a plate without bread. I felt virtuous but missed the garlic bagel as I trudged through an icy drizzle to reach the courthouse ten minutes early. When I left the elevator at the eighth floor, I saw Joe Bennett emerge from the clerk's office and amble down the hall. I followed him, and we both entered a door marked *Judge's Chambers*, which led into a ten-by-twenty-five-foot anteroom. It was brightly lit by fluorescent fixtures, and the single window at the end faced an air shaft. There were four scarred wooden visitors' chairs against the right-hand wall next to the entrance. Ten feet up, a steel secretarial desk cut across the width of the room; to the left of it stood a door that I assumed led into Judge Carter's chambers. There was no one behind the desk, so we hung our coats on a tree to the right of it, seated ourselves, and ignored each other. Five minutes later, the door opened and a woman in a hooded yellow rain slicker came in. When she hung it up, she revealed herself to be a very pretty woman with flame red hair, wearing a stylish sage suit.

"Can I help you gentlemen?"

"We're here for a conference with Judge Carter," I replied.

"On the McGrath Estate," Bennett added.

She peeked through the side door. "The judge isn't back from lunch yet," she reported, and took her seat behind the desk.

Ten minutes later a buzzer sounded. "Yes, Judge. The lawyers on the McGrath Estate are here. . . . Yes, sir. . . . Judge Carter will be with you shortly."

Five minutes later, the buzzer sounded again. "Yes, Judge, I'll send them in."

As I entered the chambers I had a strong feeling of *deja vu*: They were almost identical to those of my former boss, Judge Howard McCann—an immense room, probably thirty feet square; to the right of the entrance stood the judge's desk, a dark wooden rectangle eight feet by four, and behind him three windows facing the street. A twelve-foot conference table, and shelves containing an extensive law library on three sides, occupied the left of the room. On the remaining wall, three more windows faced the air shaft. The judge was seated behind the desk, jacket off, collar open, tie loose, smoking a curved stem pipe that looked as if it had been inherited from Judge McCann.

"Have a seat, gentlemen," he said. "As you can see, the no-smoking rule does not apply to my chambers, so you may light up."

We both declined. I noticed that the judge seemed to be less overweight than at our last conference and wondered whether smoking had reduced his appetite. Maybe I should take up the habit.

"Well, Mr. Elkins," he began after we had seated ourselves. "Mr. Bennett has accused you of sabotaging his deposition of the proponent. What do you have to say for yourself?"

"Judge, I walked out of the deposition because he was abusing my client."

"That's a *lie*!" Bennett shouted.

The judge glared at him. "Counselor, that word addressed to a fellow attorney is not to be used in my presence."

"Judge, would you please look at the last three pages of my client's deposition?" I said, handing them over. "They clearly show the abuse."

Carter read the pages, then frowned as he re-lit his pipe. "Mr. Bennett, your adversary is perfectly correct. What you did was clearly high-handed abuse."

"But—"

The judge held up his hand before turning to me. "But, Mr. Elkins, while I fully agree that not only your client but also you were being abused, that's not the way to respond to the situation. You should have recessed the examination and come to me for relief."

"I'm sorry, Your Honor. It won't happen again."

The judge nodded. "I am going to direct that your client appear for the resumption of her examination—but *please* understand, Mr. Bennett, I will not tolerate those tactics from you."

"Yes, Your Honor," Bennett replied. After musing a moment he continued, "Shouldn't my clients be compensated for Mr. Elkins's misconduct?"

With a shocked expression, the judge shook his head and turned back to me. "Let's get to the second issue. Mr. Bennett has accused you of forging the will. What do you have to say for yourself?"

"It's ridiculous."

"And not true?"

"Absolutely not."

Carter turned back to Bennett. "Are you really accusing a fellow lawyer of forgery?"

"Yes, sir."

"How do you intend to prove it?"

"So far, it's only what I truly believe, but I'd like to opportunity to get sufficient evidence."

"And you think Mr. Elkins will admit it on your examination?"

"Probably not, but I'd like the opportunity to examine him. I'm sure it will lead to evidence that will prove it."

The judge shook his head. "Okay, I allow the examination. But I don't want any abusive tactics."

"I wouldn't do that, Judge."

"You'd better not, or it will cost you. Now, do you gentlemen need a written order?"

"No, Your Honor," I replied. "I'll work out the date with Mr. Bennett. I have something to bring up, too."

"What's that?"

"I also noticed examinations of Mr. Bennett's clients."

"And?"

"They were supposed to be held the same day, but he refused to let me examine."

"Well, Mr. Bennett?"

"They were scheduled *after* I finished my examination of his side."

"Okay," said the judge. "You can start on the objectants as soon as Mr. Bennett finishes with your client."

"What about my examination of Mr. Elkins?"

"That will come after Mr. Elkins finishes with your people."

Bennett was about to nod when he thought of something else. "Judge, there's a problem."

"What's that?"

"My clients both live out of state. They were here when I deposed the witnesses and started with Ms. Keller, but they've gone back home."

"So?"

"There'll be considerable cost and inconvenience in bringing them up, and there's really no purpose for examining them. At the very least, Mr. Elkins's client should pay for their transportation and expenses."

". . .Why is there no purpose?"

"They don't have any personal knowledge of what happened with this so-called will."

I was about to speak when the judge cut in. "That's information Mr. Elkins is entitled to get, and he should be able to learn about their relationship with the testator. If you had a problem with bringing your clients up again, you should have thought about it when they were here and allowed Mr. Elkins to examine then."

"But, Your Honor—"

"I've made my decision, Mr. Bennett."

As we left the judge's chambers, neither of us was smiling.

Two hours later, Mark Rooney was at tea. Rosie had ordered up, from the local Italian restaurant, three cannoli overflowing with filling and a cappuccino topped with a generous mound of whipped cream and a few shakes of cinnamon. The repast was, alas, creating a cleaning bill for his gray flannel jacket and blue-and-yellow rep tie, for which Kathy would kill him. The intercom buzzed. "Yes, Rosie?"

"No, it's me, Mark," I answered. "You have a few minutes?"

"Sure thing, kid. Come right over."

I appeared with a cup of plain black coffee in one hand and my briefcase in the other.

"Just get back from court?" he asked as I seated myself. I nodded.

"How'd it go?"

I gave him a thumbs-down.

"McGrath?"

I nodded again.

"What happened?"

As I took a sip of my coffee, Rooney pointed to the dish of cannoli. I shook it off. "I'm having dinner at my in-laws. Got to save room."

Rooney shrugged. "You're lucky. Kathy's old lady could ruin a pot of boiled water. So?"

"The judge smiled nicely, then zapped me."

"How?"

"Told me I shouldn't have walked out of the deposition. Ordered me to bring Alice back for another shot."

"I told you so," Rooney replied, biting into his first pastry. "You've got to keep that Jewish temper of yours under control."

I nodded.

"Was that all?"

I shook my head. "He ordered me to be deposed."

"What the fuck for?"

"To prove that I didn't forge the will."

"Oh, yes, I remember. I thought the judge kaboshed it."

"I thought so, too. What should I do?"

"Let him depose you. You didn't *do* anything."

"Yeah," I replied, taking a sip of coffee. "But there's a

problem."

Rooney was startled. "Don't tell me you *did*."

I laughed. "No, but the bitch testified that I'd *repre-sented* her and her sister for a long time."

"That's bullshit. What did she mean by that?"

I described my discussion with Alice.

"Get the affidavit before either one of you testifies again."

I nodded. "I guess that's the best I can do."

"By the way, Rosie tells me Alice's already gone through the retainer, and she owes us a bundle. When you see her, put the pressure on for more money."

"I've spoken to her about it."

"And?"

"And she's afraid of dipping into the till for more until the matter is settled."

"You'd better tell her that she either comes up with more scratch or we'll have to move to be relieved as counsel."

LATE THE FOLLOWING MONDAY NIGHT, the regular monthly Metropolitan Surrogate's Association meeting was winding down. As usual, it was being held at a restaurant chosen by the current president, Frank Cornell, the Rockland County Surrogate. The restaurant wasn't always in the county where the president sat, and Cornell, having eclectic tastes, had chosen Caravela, a fine Portuguese restaurant in Tarrytown.

The Bronx Surrogate, George Stevens, the association vice-president, had arrived at six, had a Black Bush on the rocks, and shot the breeze with his colleagues until six-thirty, when they sat down to dinner: garlic sausages, a salad, and a whole sea bass accompanied by sauteed spinach and fried potatoes; he polished off half a bottle of a Portuguese red as he surgically separated the fish from its skeleton. He finished with coffee, avoiding the rich desserts for dietary reasons. The program featured his report on proposed changes of personal service requirements under the Surrogates Court Procedure Act. The report was well received: the association endorsed his recommendation to reject the changes as unnecessary. After the meeting adjourned, he ordered more coffee to guard against the possible consequences of driving home with an excessive blood alcohol level.

"Great report, George. You're going to make a hell of a president next year."

Stevens started. "Oh, hi, Al. I thought I was the last one here."

Albert Carter shook his head.

"Join me." Stevens pointed to the pot and two extra cups.

"Thanks." Carter poured a cup and added two artificial

sweeteners.

They drank their coffee in near silence. Stevens ordered another pot. Finally, the Westchester Surrogate spoke up. "I'm glad you stayed late. I wanted to have a private word with you."

"Oh? You recruiting me to be your campaign manager when you run for the Court of Appeals?"

"From your lips to God's ears."

They both chuckled.

"So? What's up?"

"It's a disturbing matter that I spoke to you about before. That young man, Ian Elkins, you recommended to me."

"Yes, a very nice, bright young lawyer. You'd told me someone accused him of forging a will?"

"Yes, and you'd told me it couldn't possibly be true."

"It can't. The kid is a boy scout. He wouldn't even take advantage of a dinner bill that wasn't added right. What happened?"

"It came up again."

"Someone *else* accused him?" Stevens asked with a troubled expression.

"No. Same lawyer, same case."

"Who was it?"

"Joseph Bennett."

Stevens knitted his brow. "Oh, yeah, I remember him.

He used to represent those Iron Curtain claimants. They're a sleazy bunch. . . . You don't believe it—do you?"

Carter shook his head but retained a troubled look.

"What is it, Al?"

"Why would a lawyer make such an outrageous charge unless there was at least a germ of truth in it?"

Stevens offered no response.

"You realize I can't give him any appointments until this is straightened out?"

Stevens shrugged and nodded.

CHAPTER ELEVEN

THE FOLLOWING WEDNESDAY EVENING was the first time Alice was available to see me. I got there promptly at nine, grumbling to myself that she wouldn't make it earlier and wondering how I'd gotten stuck with her. She led me into the living room, where she was working on her second after-dinner drink. "Can I get you something?" she asked coquettishly.

I shook my head, then changed my mind. "A glass of ice water would be nice," I replied mopping my brow. "Why do you keep the place so hot?"

She smiled. "It's the fucking tenants. They held a rent strike, claiming we didn't give enough heat. So we're really giving it to them now."

"Can't you turn it down in *your* apartment?"

"I've tried," she replied, shaking her head. "It doesn't work like that."

When she returned with my water, I reached into my briefcase and pulled out a two-page affidavit. "This is what I put together from your comments on the transcript to your examination. Does it cover everything?"

She took a sip of her drink, read quickly. "It'll do."

"Is it complete and right?" I snapped.

"I said it would *do!*"

"Damn it, Alice, it's got to be complete and accurate. Is it?"

"Yes, and stop yelling at me."

"Then *cooperate*."

She shrugged. "I'm sorry. I know you're trying to do the best for me."

"Okay, now sign the affidavit."

She did, and I put it in my file and pulled out the original of the transcript, which she also signed.

"Now we'd better go over your testimony. Remember, we're on for this Friday."

"Why the hell do I have to be there?" she said, her eyes blazing. "I can't waste my time. I've got too much work to do."

"Because the court says so, and you didn't do yourself any good by testifying that I knew Moira."

"You know why. It's in my affidavit. I got a little nervous."

I shook my head. What she'd told me that I'd put into the affidavit was that I'd inspired confidence in her when we met, and she saw me as her lifetime lawyer. That feeling must have turned into a pipe dream that she had known me for a long time. She was very close to her sister, and since Moira would have taken half if she'd survived Uncle Jim, I must have been *her* lawyer as well. Bennett's accusatory questioning had shaken Alice up, and she had testified to her pipe dream. "I hope the jury believes it," I said.

"Why shouldn't they? It's the *truth*!" She slammed her glass down.

For the next forty-five minutes we discussed what I figured Bennett would ask, emphasizing that she must tell only the truth. I explored the information about her uncles for use during their depositions. Just as I was about to leave, I said, "Look, Alice—we're going to need more money now. You're over fifty-five hundred behind, and it's growing fast. These night visits at your apartment don't help."

"What can I do? I have a big business to run. I really can't take the time. Don't worry, you'll get paid."

My attitude softened. "Look, I understand, but you've got to realize we need money *now*. My firm has expenses to meet. We've got a landlord, too."

She smiled. "Don't worry, I get it. I'll bring you a check on Friday."

"The whole balance?"

". . .I'll do what I can."

THE DEPOSITIONS WERE SCHEDULED TO START at 10:00; as usual, I showed up twenty minutes early. That morning it paid off. I reached the garage so early that I had time for a plate of ham and eggs over light, and a croissant that came with it, at one of the stands in the food court. I had told myself I'd avoid the croissant, and compromised by wolfing down only half.

I seated myself at the table in the deposition room; five minutes later, the reporter arrived, this time a thin man with a pointed gray beard. "Where's Myrna?" I asked.

"She had to go to the doctor. I'm Joel Levy, her father. I used to have her job before I retired." He handed me his card. "Where's your machine?"

Levy reached into the breast pocket of his brown-checked sports jacket, removed a gold Waterman's fountain pen, and held it up. "A lot more reliable than those new-fangled gadgets," he declared. "And in these hands, just as fast."

The door opened, and Joe Bennett stormed in. "Okay, Elkins, where is she?"

I pointed to my watch. "It's five of. She'll be here."

"She'd better be."

"Where're *your* clients?" I retorted.

"They'll be here." Just then, Hal and Charlie arrived, and Bennett motioned them to seats.

"Where's the lying bitch?" Hal rasped.

I was about to make a brash retort, exhibiting confidence I didn't have, when the door opened and Alice swept in. She removed her white beaver coat, laid it on one of the chairs, put her purse on the table, and asked for the ladies room.

"Down the hall to your right," Levy told her.

"And don't take all day," Bennett added.

Charlie snickered.

"Who does he think he is," she asked me, "my urologist?" and left.

During Alice's absence, I gave Bennett her signed deposition transcript and affidavit, which he tossed carelessly aside. This surprised me, since, had the tables been turned, I would have been reading it furiously. Instead, the young man spent the next five minutes in whispered conference with his clients. Then he turned to me. "What the hell's keeping her? She should have peed before she left home."

I looked at him and shook my head. For the next ten minutes Bennett continued his conversation with the Mc-Graths.

"What the hell *kept* you?" he demanded when Alice finally returned.

"If I'd known you were that interested," she replied, "I would have invited you along to watch."

Charlie started to giggle but stopped when Hal glared at him.

Bennett turned to the reporter. "Okay, swear her in."

"You don't have to do that," I interjected. "This is a continued examination. All you need is to remind her that she's still under oath."

"Well, swear her in anyway," Bennett replied with a sneer. "That way maybe she'll tell the truth this time."

Alice was about to respond when I held up my hand. "Mr. Bennett, Judge Carter specifically ordered you not to abuse my client. If you continue with unwarranted attack, we'll have to go in an see him now."

Bennett's face reddened. "You're reminded that you're still under oath. Do you understand?"

Alice nodded.

"Respond in *words*!"

"She said yes," I told him.

"Have her *say* it."

"Yes," Alice said, repressing a laugh.

"Okay, let's get started. When did you forge your uncle's will?"

"I didn't."

"Answer the question."

"She did," I said.

"No, she didn't," Bennett retorted, and turned to the reporter. "Mark that for a ruling."

Levy lifted his gold pen high into the air and brought it down to the paper with a flourish.

Bennett gritted his teeth. "When did you instruct your lawyer to forge the will?"

"I didn't."

"Answer the question."

"She did."

"Okay, Elkins, I've taken enough of your crap. Let's go see the judge."

I shrugged and spread my palms, then turned to Alice. "Please wait here while this kid has his tantrum."

"How *dare* you!" Bennett exclaimed.

"I always tell the truth. Come on, sonny, let's get it over with."

We went to the waiting room of the judge's chambers and asked to see him. When his secretary learned the purpose of our visit, she sent us to the judge's law secretary. "Mr. McCullough takes care of rulings," she explained. We left the anteroom and turned down the hall to a door marked *Frank McCullough, Law Secretary.*

We entered a fifteen-square-foot room. with one window facing the street. The walls on both sides were lined with steel bookshelves. Facing us behind a cluttered desk, with his back to the single window overlooking the street, sat a man in his late twenties with curly blonde hair and a full blonde beard. The collar of his striped shirt was open, as was his gray tweed vest, and his blue-and-red rep tie was unknotted. "Can I help you?" he asked.

When we explained the purpose of our visit, Bennett started to give him background. The law secretary held up his hand. "Joel, please read me the transcript." After the reporter complied, McCullough looked at Bennett in disbelief, scratched his beard, and turned to me. "Mr. Elkins, he's technically right."

Bennett smiled broadly.

"Mr. Bennett's questions called for a time, not whether she forged the will or had you do it. Of course, at trial you can object to the question as assuming facts not in evidence, but for now she must answer."

"But how can she fix a time for something that didn't happen?" I asked, puzzled.

"Have you heard of the word 'never'?"

I smiled; Bennett's grin turned into a scowl.

When I told Alice, Bennett objected to my "coaching the witness." Shortly thereafter, the lawyer for the objectants went on to a different topic. He asked about Moira's death and about how long I had represented her before she died. When Alice replied that neither she nor Moira had ever *met* me before Moira's death, Bennett opened the transcript of her original deposition and asked, "Ms. Keller, at the last session, didn't you testify that Mr. Elkins represented your sister and you?"

I muttered, "It's in the affidavit, Mr. Bennett."

"Stop interrupting, Elkins. What affidavit?"

"The affidavit I *gave* you, along with my client's signed examination."

Bennett reached for the discarded papers and read. Then he slapped his palms on the table. "Who the hell made up this bullshit?" he demanded.

"It's the truth."

"Come off it. Did you do it, Elkins?"

I ignored him.

"Answer the question."

"I'm not the witness."

He turned back to Alice. "Did he do this?"

"He prepared the affidavit," she answered, knitting her brow.

"So your lawyer made this *up*," he concluded, a broad smile on his face. "I'm going to enjoy getting him disbarred."

"That's not what she said, Mr. Bennett. She told me the facts, and I prepared the affidavit. Don't tell me your clients do their own typing," I said, eying Hal.

"I thought you weren't testifying, Elkins."

"I'm not. Ask *her* the question."

"Don't tell me what to do!"

"Suit yourself," I replied with a shrug.

For the next five minutes, Bennett reread the affidavit carefully. Then he looked directly into Alice's eyes. "No jury's going to believe that."

"We'll see," I replied. "Have you finished with the Petitioner?" I asked after he spent the next five minutes staring a notes he had made on a yellow legal pad.

"Yeah. She's not going to tell the truth."

"Okay," I said to the reporter. "Please swear in Mr. Harold McGrath."

For the next two and a half hours, I conducted a meticulous examination of the McGrath brothers. While little useful information emerged, I got Hal to admit he'd had very little contact with his older brother since graduating from college fifteen years before, in fact hadn't seen him in person since the post-graduation party. Charlie admitted Jim had fired him after it was discovered that he was receiving gifts from suppliers, including a diamond-encrusted gold Rolex from the exclusive electrical contractor for the real estate company. Both brothers conceded that the only thing they knew about the claimed will forgery came from their handwriting expert.

After the examinations ended, Alice and I started for the door. "Where the hell are you going?" Bennett demanded, pointing to me. "I'm ready to examine *you*."

"To confer with my client."

"So she can tell you what to say?"

"Grow up, kid," I replied as we left.

When we were alone in the hall, I asked her whether she wanted to stay for my deposition. She declined, saying she was too busy. "You're probably right," I commented. "Before you go, where's the check?

She returned to the room, grabbed her coat and purse, and again left. In the hall she handed me a sealed envelope. I tore it open in anticipation; then my face fell. "Only seven fifty?" "That's all I can afford now."

"You'll have to do better than that," I said and went back in.

"Okay, wise guy forger, now we'll have some fun." Bennett chortled.

I gave Bennett an amazed look then turned to the reporter. "Have you gotten that down, Mr. Levy?"

"No, but I have it now," the reporter replied, making a note on his pad.

"Wait a minute!" Bennett shouted. "That's not part of the examination."

"Oh, yes it is," I replied with a smile. "Get all of this, Mr. Levy."

"Cross that *out*," Bennett barked. "I'm not going to pay for that."

"Let's talk to Frank McCullough," I retorted.

Bennett waved his hand. "Okay, swear him in." For the next hour he questioned me exhaustively about my history and background. He went through my education from high school through college and law school. He explored my seven years at the surrogate's court law department, questioned me carefully about my outside cases, and seemed disappointed when I answered that I'd *had* no outside cases, because Judge McCann discouraged it.

"But all the other law assistants have some outside practice."

"Not in Howard McCann's court."

Bennett next went into my practice after I left the court and finally got to Alice. "Well, didn't you have any contact with your client or her family before you were retained for this estate?"

"With her family, a little."

"Ah!" Bennett declared with a smile. "Now we're getting somewhere. What contact *did* you have? When? And with whom?"

I explained about my landlord-and-tenant cases against McGrath's company.

Finally, Bennett gave up and closed the examination, and the McGraths immediately picked up and left. "We've got planes to catch," said Hal as he waddled through the door.

As we were packing up, my curiosity got the better of

me. "Tell me, Bennett, why are you trying to bust my chops?"

"What's the matter, can't you take it?"

"Sure I can, but what's the *point*?"

"Because you deserve it."

"What did I ever do to *you*?" I asked.

"Plenty. I don't like you holier-than-thou boys. I've always figured you've got a skeleton in the closet, and I'm going to find it."

"How am I holier than thou?"

"Look what you used to do to me when you were a referee."

"I didn't do *anything* to you. I just made you prove your case. Did I ever rule against any of your claimants?"

"No, but you made me bust my ass."

I shook my head. "It was my *job* to see that you did *your* job. If I'd just let everything slide, the judge would have canned me, and he would have been right."

Bennett hesitated for a moment while he packed his file into a litigation case with wheels. "How about Justin Taylor? You got him disbarred, and he almost went to prison."

"Oh, come on, *he* did that to himself. He had a phony case on forged documents—and he had a hit man who almost *killed* me. He was damned *lucky* he didn't go to jail. That doesn't justify you making a bullshit claim that I forged a will. You know it isn't true."

"Don't worry, I'll prove it."

"Let me give you a piece of advice," I said as I put my file into an expandable canvas brief case. "Accusing me of forging the will is hurting your case."

"...How?"

"You're wasting a lot of time and money on a phony claim. Unless you have solid proof, you'll never get it before the jury."

"Oh, I'll get it there."

I was beginning to think I was wasting my time. It was after two, and my stomach was growling, but I'd started, so I'd finish it. "If you do, you'll be *worse* off. Either the judge will grant a mistrial, or, if he doesn't, the jury is going to hear a phony charge that you can't back up and figure anything else you say is a lot of crap."

Bennett laughed as he departed, but he was troubled. I was right. How was he going to explain to Hal that he would have to drop his claim against me?

CHAPTER
TWELVE

HAT FRIDAY EVENING, THE GOLDSTEINS were away skiing; only Helen and I joined her parents for dinner. Molly had wanted Helen's obstetrician to check the sonogram so she could know whether to knit in pink or blue, but Helen was insistent on being surprised. Actually, she'd had tried to beg off that night—there was a movie we'd wanted to see—but Molly had insisted that her grandchild had to be well nourished.

The dining room table was, as usual, set formally with Molly's best china, a linen tablecloth, and lit candles. Molly did the serving—fresh fruit cups, salad, and the main course. Ian asked, "That looks and smells great, Mom. What is it?"

"Arroz con pollo *a la Havana.*"

"Very fancy," Sam added.

"Where'd you find the recipe?" Helen asked.

"Sadie Miller gave me a book. *Food of the Islands.*"

"What's in it?"

"First you cut up a whole chicken in small pieces. Then you marinate it in garlic and beer for three days. Then, just before you got here, I sauteed it and added rice and wine and, at the last minute, peas and pimentos."

Afterwards Molly brought in a dark chocolate cake with white icing, and cut four slices. "That's too big for him," Helen declared, as Molly passed the largest piece to me.

"Oh come on," Sam said. "He works hard and needs his nourishment."

"He's *too fat*," she replied to no avail as I took my first mouthful.

"Join me for a brandy with your coffee, Ian?" Sam asked as the group sat down in the living room. "Good for the digestion."

"No thanks, Dad. I've got to drive your daughter and grandchild home in a little while."

"And *you* shouldn't either, Sam," Molly insisted. "Remember what the doctor said."

"Oh? What does the doctor know? I've been doing this for years."

"What's the matter with him, Mom?" Helen asked with

a look of concern.

"There's nothing the matter, and I'm feeling just fine. The doctor is an old lady."

Helen continued to look at her mother.

"It's nothing specific," Molly explained, "but the doctor told him to lose at least twenty pounds and cut down on his drinking."

"Aw, cutting out the good things in life won't make me live longer. It'll just *seem* longer. Tell me, Ian, what's new in the office? How's that famous case going?"

"You *see?*" Molly exclaimed. "He's changing the topic. He never listens."

"Why shouldn't a man be interested in his son-in-law's career?"

She silently shook her head.

"So?"

"Not too good, Dad. I got a real kick in the ass today."

"What happened?" asked Helen with a worried look.

"It's the money. The litigation's going hot and heavy. The client's run through her retainer, and she's into us for a lot of dough."

"So bill her," Sam advised.

"We bill every month."

"Can't you tell her to pay up?" Molly asked.

"I have. In fact, I read her the riot act on Wednesday night."

Sam frowned. "And?"

"She keeps telling me money's tight, and she can't take much out of her uncle's business until we win the case."

"What if you lose, and she *doesn't* get the money?" Molly asked with a look of alarm.

"She'll still have plenty. She gets a quarter of the estate anyway."

"Then it's okay," Molly said with a sigh.

"Not really. In the first place, we need continuing income to cover our expenses, and even if we *could* carry the case to the end, if we lose, we're in big trouble."

Molly looked puzzled.

"If they lose," said Sam, "The client's not going to be willing to pay much."

I nodded. "And if we have to sue, she's going to counterclaim for malpractice."

"So what are you going to do?" asked Helen.

"When I saw her on Wednesday, I told her we'd have to have a check by today or we wanted to be relieved. She gave me a check today . . . for a lousy seven-fifty."

"So?" Sam prodded.

"So I had a meeting with Mark when I got back to the office today."

"What does he think?"

"He ordered me to tell Alice that, if she didn't pay at least half the outstanding balance within a week and then keep current, we're going to make a motion to be relieved."

"That Irishman you work for has a good head on his shoulders."

"It's not that easy. In the first place, the court may not let us off the hook. They frequently don't when you're this far into a case."

"And the second?" Helen asked.

Sam chuckled. "He doesn't *want* to let go of a big case."

My red face confirmed that Sam had hit the nail on the head.

THE FOLLOWING FRIDAY, I WAS SUMMONED into the boss's room. As I seated myself, I looked at Mark and almost broke up. "What happened to the cappuccino and cannolis? I thought today was Friday."

Rooney chuckled, then deliberately reached into a box of Famous Amos chocolate chip cookies, withdrew one, and took a big bite. "It's good to see my staff is observant about some things."

"So give."

The big man blushed. "It's Kathy. She's pissed at me for ruining good ties on the whipped cream and cannoli filling," he replied, taking a sip of coffee lightened by heavy cream. "But that's not why I called you in."

"I didn't think so. What's up?"

"McGrath. When are we getting our fucking dough?"

"I wish I knew."

"Didn't you speak to her like I told you last week.?"

"I did." I nodded feeling dejected. "It didn't make a dent. I had to call her five times before I got her in, and I couldn't get a definite answer."

"You ought to write her," Rooney barked, chewing furiously.

"I did," I replied, handing over a copy of my letter with a certified mail receipt attached.

Rooney read it slurping coffee. He shook his head. "Good letter. I couldn't have done better myself."

"What's next?"

"Call her when you get the receipt."

"And?"

"Depends on what she says. If she promises a substantial check in a reasonable time, we've got to wait."

"Otherwise we make the motion?"

"Not quite. I've done this before, and there are some steps you've got to take first."

I dropped my legal pad on Rooney's desk and pulled a pen from my shirt pocket.

"First, tell her to get a substitute attorney, and follow it up with another certified letter giving her thirty days to get one. The letter has to say that, if she doesn't get the replacement within the time, you'll make the motion."

"And in the meantime, what do I do? Sit on my hands?"

Rooney shook his head. "No way, kid. We don't need a malpractice claim. During the interim you give her the same service she'd get if she was a paying client. After the thirty days run, ask Rosie for the Mazolla file. There's a motion to be relieved in there."

As I left Rooney's office, I mused—why the hell didn't I go back to the court system when I had the chance?

"WHO THE FUCK IS THIS?" Alice was annoyed at the 9:45 phone call.

"It's me, Alice."

"Why so late?"

"Cause you don't return calls."

"So what's up?"

"Money. You got my letter."

"You'll get paid, but I don't have it right now."

"Then you've got to get yourself another lawyer."

"I don't *need* another lawyer. I've got *you*. Just a minute," she said, putting a hand over the mouthpiece and turning to Les, who was lying next to her in the bed. "What do I do?"

He spread his open palms. "Tell him you're not going to let him go."

"Look, Ian, I'm not going to get another lawyer."

"Then I'll have to make a motion to be relieved."

"What's that?"

I explained. "Wait a minute," she replied, and covered the mouthpiece again. "He says he's going to make a motion to the court, and either I'll have to get a new lawyer or not have one."

"So let him. The judge will never let him out of the case this late in the game."

"I'm sorry, Ian, but I can't let you go. You'll just have to do what you have to do," she concluded, and hung up.

CHAPTER THIRTEEN

"YOU GOT A CALL, HAL," CAROL MCGRATH told her husband as he lumbered into the living room.

"Who the fuck was it?"

"Won't you please stop using that language?" She was still gazing out the window at the sunset.

"For Christ's sake, what language?"

"And please don't take the Lord's name in vain. Maybe if you didn't drink so much—"

"Aw, I only had a few cold ones at Scully's—and come to think of it, who're *you* to talk?" he replied, pointing to the frosted glass on the table next to her rocker.

"I was thirsty," she answered, blushing.

"I'll bet." He sniffed the glass. "Smells like gin to me. Who called?"

"Your lawyer, Bennett."

"What'd he want?"

"He didn't say. He just said for you to call him." She took a sip of her Tom Collins.

Hal got himself a bottle of Busch from the refrigerator, poured it into a frozen mug from the freezer, returned to the living room, and sat down on a monster-sized easy chair next to the phone.

"Please, Hal, put a coaster under the glass. You'll ruin the table."

He waved dismissively and picked up the phone. "Hi, Joe. What's up?" he said when the lawyer got on the line. "...That's great. Good job." He hung up.

"What is it?" Carol asked as she returned from the kitchen with her second refill.

"We beat the bitch!" he announced triumphantly.

"Alice dropped her case?"

"Not yet, but soon. Her fucking lawyer just made a motion to get out. He says she's not paying him."

THAT WEEK THE LAW DEPARTMENTS of New York Metropolitan Area Surrogates Courts held one of their required continuing legal education seminars. This one was at the Tarrytown Marriott. After the session Bill Anderson had lunch with his friend Sam Bonas, who headed the law department in Westchester. As they were sipping their coffee, Bill asked, "Sam, can I ask you a question out of school?"

"About what?"

"A case that's before your judge now."

"You can ask. I may not be able to help you, but I won't hold it against you."

"It's about a friend of mine," Anderson continued, blushing slightly. "A nice young lawyer who used to work for me."

"Elkins?"

Bill nodded. "I understand it's a motion to be relieved. The kid's kind of nervous. His firm isn't being paid."

"I know all about it. In fact I was in the courtroom when it was being argued."

"Any chance of him getting off the hook?"

Bonas shook his head. "If it were my decision, I'd let him out even if he weren't a friend of yours. None of us like that son of a bitch Bennett—not even the judge. Can you imagine accusing another lawyer of *forging a will?*"

"Then. . . ?"

"Another judge might, but my boss wants to move cases. That'll be the reason for denying the motion. Too close to trial."

"What kind of representation can you expect from a

lawyer who isn't being paid?"

"It's a memory problem. Al Carter's been on the bench for over twenty years. He can't remember the time when he needed to collect a fee to pay the rent and feed his family."

A WEEK AND A HALF LATER, I RECEIVED a copy of the court's decision. While it expressed sympathy, it concluded that, in the words of the great Justice Arthur Vanderbilt, "justice delayed is justice denied," and the case had been pending too long. The decision set a trial date for two months hence and directed the parties to exchange expert reports within two weeks and conclude the depositions of the experts within a month thereafter.

At 10:30 the following night, I was finally able to reach Alice on the phone.

"Must you *always* call me late at night?" she demanded.

"Alice cut the bullshit."

". . .What is it?"

"The judge decided the motion—"

"I know. He sent me a copy."

"So where's our expert's report?"

"How should *I* know? You're the lawyer. That's your job."

"Now, look, Alice—when I *wanted* to consult an expert, you said not to, that you'd get one. Do we have an expert, or don't we?"

"You *know* we have one. Didn't I give you his name and background?"

"Sure, and when I wanted to interview him, you told me don't worry, when the time comes I would."

"So?"

"The time's come. Where is he?"

". . .I'll let you know."

"When?"

"Soon. Stop being a pain in the ass."

"Soon's not good enough. I need him *right now*."

"I'll call you."

"When?"

". . . Tomorrow."

As I hung up , I was reconsidering life as a court attorney. Those had been simpler times.

THE FOLLOWING MORNING, ALGERNON FLYNN was skimming through the day's surrogate's court decisions in the *Law Journal* when his intercom buzzed. "Yes, Maureen."

"Mr. Donovan wants to see you in his office."

"I'll be right in," he replied, gulping down the balance of his third cup of coffee. He laid the blue-patterned china cup and saucer on the pullout slide of his desk, grabbed his jacket from the hook behind his door, and strode out. A few moments later he was seated in a tan leather visitor's chair in front of the managing partner's oval desk.

"Coffee, my boy?" Donovan asked, fingering the Phi Delta Phi law school key that hung from a thin gold chain across his open vest.

"Yes, thank you, sir."

"Thelma, bring in coffee and some of those nice sticky buns that came in today."

A few minutes later a tray with a thermal carafe, a blue-patterned china creamer with matching cups and saucers, and a plate of buns was brought in by a tall, slightly plump matron in a powder-blue three-piece suit. Thelma Regan had been Donovan's secretary for over twenty years and knew how to take care of him.

The lawyers made small talk while they sipped their coffee and Donovan demolished three of the sticky buns. After they had commiserated with each other on the poor season the Knicks were having, Donovan finally said, "The Cardinal's been asking me about our progress in the McGrath Estate. What can I tell him?"

As the young man pondered his answer, he looked up at the autographed portrait of Pope John Paul I, a rarity considering his short tenure in the holy office. "We're not doing too well so far, sir. I have an investigator looking for the later will that Mrs. Curran believes he made."

"Curran?"

"That's Mr. McGrath's sister. She's the nun's mother."

Donovan nodded. "How's the search going?"

"Nothing yet, but these things take time."

"What about the will the niece submitted for probate?"

"It's a problem, sir," Flynn replied with a near grimace. "They're using a fellow named Mario Gambi as their handwriting expert. He doesn't have the greatest reputation."

The managing partner looked dolefully at his associate. "Algernon, as you know, we will soon be considering your class of associates for partnership."

Flynn had trouble avoiding a fearful expression.

"If you can pull this off, you'll have a good future with this firm." Donovan didn't need to mention the alternative.

"THAT WAS THE BEST MEAL I'VE HAD in months, Mother. The lamb stew was super, and there's nobody who makes an apple pie like you do."

"Let me cut you another small slice with a dab more ice cream, Mary Elizabeth," replied a beaming Mary Curran.

The young nun shook her head. "Thanks, but I can't eat a bite more. If I take another mouthful I'll split a seam, and that might create a scandal." She pointed to the tight fitting jeans she had exchanged for her habit when she got home.

Both mother and daughter laughed. "It wouldn't do any harm for you to gain a few pounds. A sister doesn't have to look like a bathing beauty."

"If it's all the same to you, Mom, I think I'll just let nature take its course," the nun replied, remembering how much she and her mother had looked alike before twenty years and thirty pounds had turned a model into a matron. Weight was the curse of the McGrath family. She was lucky that good looks weren't one of her job requirements. Over her mother's protest, Mary Elizabeth cleared the table, washed the pot, and loaded the dishwasher.

"I'll bet you have a much better kitchen at the convent."

"It's a lot bigger, but we can't afford all this modern equipment. Besides, we've got a lot more mouths to feed."

"That's what I meant. I've always hated this kitchen. It's so narrow. I always wanted an eat-in one."

"Eating in the dining room isn't so bad. In fact, it's sort of elegant," Mary Elizabeth pointed out as the two women refilled their coffee cups and entered the living room.

They sat together on a worn couch, listening to a Bach fugue on the CD player. They enjoyed each other's company and looked forward to the occasional weekends when Mary Elizabeth was able to come home from the convent. When the music stopped, they reminisced about her growing up and when Daddy was alive. Mary Elizabeth went to the kitchen and brought back more coffee and a peach-pie and ice-cream refill for her mother.

Afterwards Mary noticed that her daughter was eying her expectantly.

"What is it, dear?"

The young nun blushed. "I was just wondering whether you'd heard anything about Uncle Jim's estate. Mother Superior asked me to speak to you—the repairs, you know."

"Nothing new."

"Didn't that lawyer, Flynn, call you? I told him to."

"Oh, yes, he called, but all he did was ask me more questions about a *later* will."

"Did you remember anything?"

"Just a little more. I remember Jim told me about his lawyer. A little Jewish fellow from the Bronx."

"Did you remember his name?"

The older woman shook her head.

"Did Mr. Flynn tell you anything about how the case was going?"

"Just that it's near trial."

"What do you think of him?"

"I don't like him, dear."

"That's funny, neither do I. He's too smooth. I don't trust him."

CHAPTER FOURTEEN

I
T TOOK ME OVER A WEEK to get in touch with my handwriting expert. I'd both written and phoned the man. All my calls had triggered a phone message beginning with fifteen seconds of hard rock followed by "I ain't in, man. Leave a message." After eight messages in three days, I added Alice to my call list. I finally got her in at home at ten-thirty on a Thursday evening. After her usual grousing about late night calls, she promised to get the expert to call me, and at five-thirty on Monday the call finally came.

"What you bothering me for, man?"

"I wrote you a week ago, Mr. Gambi. My letter gives you the exact detail of the report we need from you."

"If you wrote me, why you calling me?"

"Because I need that report now."

"That's gonna take a whole lotta work. I'm busy now."

"I need to have it in my hands by this Thursday at the latest."

"If I'm going to drop everything to do this, it's gotta cost."

". . .How much?"

"Send me five Gs on account."

I cogitated as I watched the flickering fluorescent light over my desk and thought I really should get it changed. "That's way out of line. You'd better talk to Ms. Keller."

"Who?"

"Alice Keller."

"Oh, *Alice*," he replied, and hung up.

On Tuesday I received a call from Alice. "What the hell did you do?"

"What're you talking about?"

"Did you set me up to pay Mario five thousand dollars?"

"No. I told him I thought that was way out of line, but that he should call you. I guess he did."

"Okay, I'll take care of him. What will you need?"

"A report giving the details of his expert testimony, including his qualifications, what he concluded, why, and what he'll testify to."

"I'll have him send it to you."

"Look, Alice, I've got to have it in my hands no later

than this Thursday, so I can serve a copy on Joe Bennett."

"Don't worry, you will."

On THURSDAY, MUCH TO MY SURPRISE, I received the report, which came pretty close to complying with the rules. I served it on Bennett and, a few days later, received the report of the other side's expert. Read in a vacuum, each would have convinced a reader that its side was correct and the other way out of line. Both Bennett and I served notices for depositions and, as a matter of convenience agreed to an examination date at the courthouse two Mondays thence.

I generally try to have my witness come to my office to prepare testimony, but Gambi insisted it had to be in *his* office, and at night. So on the Thursday evening before the examination date, I made my way to lower Manhattan. The building was mainly tenanted as a low-class lawyer's building, and, while the public areas had recently been refurbished, that message still came through. Gambi had told me he was in Suite 1051, on the tenth floor, but when I got there his name wasn't on the directory. The door was locked, and I had to ring a buzzer. After about five minutes the door was opened by a tall Asian wearing a double-breasted vest over a tieless white shirt. "Yeah?" he asked.

"I have an appointment to see Mr. Gambi."

"Who?"

"Mario Gambi."

"Oh, Mario. Wait a minute. I thought I saw him around."

I took a seat on one of several mismatched visitor's chairs and skimmed through a two-month old *People's* magazine. A few minutes later a man asked, "You waiting for me?"

"You Mr. Gambi?"

"Yeah, I'm Mario." He was tall, with curly hair, a long nose, and a waxed black mustache. He had on tight-fitting designer jeans, tasseled loafers, and a blue silk shirt. "You Alice's lawyer?"

I nodded, introduced myself and shook hands.

He led me to an eight-by-ten room with a single window overlooking an air shaft. There was a completely bare, thirty-by-sixty-inch desk backing on the window, with an ancient desk chair and a folding visitor's chair. "Hang yourself up," he said, pointing to a coat tree.

I complied, seated myself, removed a file from my briefcase, and took out the two expert reports. "I assume you read the other one."

"Yeah."

"How come they're so different?"

Gambi gave me a look you'd expect from an astronaut seeing his first Martian. "Cause if they were the same, you wouldn't need me."

I blushed. "Look, Mr. Gambi—"

"Mario."

"Mario. Explain to me why your report is right and his is wrong."

He spent the next ten minutes on what he termed "an elementary course in the science of disputed documents." By the end of the lecture I was, if anything, more confused. It involved similarity of loops, direction, pressure, size, and compactness, and stressed that you *needed* strong similarity, but that if the specimens were *too* similar, that was an indication of tracing or some other form of forgery. Gambi concluded with the admonition, "Don't worry, I know my business."

"I notice you last testified seven years ago. How is that?"

"I've been doing other kinds of work—but don't worry, my skill and experience don't go stale."

About a half hour into the meeting the Asian stuck his head into the doorway. "Mario?"

"Yeah, Tony."

"We've rented out this room for next week, so don't leave any of your crap in it."

"Sure thing."

When I left the office nearly an hour later, My confidence in my expert had been deeply shaken.

I ENTERED THE DEPOSITION ROOM that Monday morning twenty minutes early as usual. Five minutes later, fountain pen and steno book in hand, Joel Levy arrived. "Good morning, Joel."

The smiling reporter nodded and seated himself at the far end of the table.

"What happened to Myrna? Have you grabbed your old job back from her?"

"Just temporary. She's on her maternity leave, taking care of my grandson, Josh."

"Congratulations. He your first?"

"First grandson, but he has two older sisters. You have any children?"

"One on the way."

"When's he or she due?"

"About a month and a half."

"Boy or girl?"

"Don't know. My wife insists on a surprise. Helen's driving her mother crazy. She doesn't know what to knit."

Levy shrugged. "Yeah, Myrna's that way, too. My wife's got the same problem. My son and daughter-in-law are much more considerate. She's pregnant with her first, and he's already been named Jack."

"So where is he, Elkins?" Joe Bennett demanded as he came through the doorway.

"He'll be here. Where's your guy?"

"So will mine. I told him to come about eleven. Remember, I noticed you first, so I lead off."

I nodded. "I know the rules."

A few minutes later Mario Gambi wandered in. He was dressed in the same outfit he'd worn at our Thursday night meeting. I hoped that he had a suit for the trial.

Gambi was sworn in, and Bennett examined him in a leisurely fashion. He started with his education and training; then went on to his experience in the field, and finally into great detail about his examination of the will and his conclusions. Throughout the questioning, Bennett exercised a great deal of patience and courtesy.

About an hour and a half into it, Bruce Malone entered the examination room. His black calfskin jacket was open, displaying a tee shirt with the *Malone Disputed Documents* logo. Bennett introduced him, then asked him to wait outside until Gambi's examination was complete.

"Should I come back after lunch?" Malone asked.

"No, stick around. I should be done in less than a half hour."

When we all resumed our seats, a smile crossed Bennett's previously serious expression. "Now, Mr. Gambi, I notice that you haven't been doing any disputed documents work in the past seven years. Why is that?"

"I was in another business for a while."

"And what was that business?"

"Printing. I was running a printing plant."

"And where was that?"

"Upstate New York."

"Where upstate?"

"Clinton County?"

"Where in Clinton County?" Bennett's smile grew broader.

Gambi blushed and coughed.

"Perhaps I can help you, Mr. Gambi. Was the plant in Dannemora?"

Gambi nodded.

"You'll have to say 'yes' or 'no', Mr. Gambi. The reporter can't take down nonverbal responses."

"Yes," Gambi whispered.

"Was the plant in the Clinton Correctional Facility?"

"Yes."

"That's a prison, isn't it? And you were an inmate, weren't you?"

"Yes," Gambi replied, nearly gagging.

"And what were you convicted of, Mr. Gambi?"

"Fraud."

"And?"

"Perjury."

"No further questions."

As I struggled with a world collapsing about me, Gambi

tugged at my arm and led me outside. Ten minutes later, I returned to start my examination of Bruce Malone. My face was no longer ashen.

MY EXAMINATION OF MALONE PARALLELED Bennett's. In fact I had learned a few things from my adversary's questioning that I used to advantage. About an hour into the examination, Joel Levy held up his hand. "Gentlemen, we're going to have to take a break. I've been going for over three hours. My hand is tired, and I'm hungry. Why don't we break for lunch and come back in an hour?"

We agreed, and had lunch at the same coffee shop we'd lunched in during the first set of examinations. Bennett again refused to eat with me and the reporter and I ate at a separate table.

Levy asked me about Bennett's animosity towards me and commented on what happened during Gambi's examination. "He sure enjoyed zapping that witness of yours. Where'd you get that clown?"

"The client insisted on using him. I heard he wasn't the greatest, but I never imagined he was a jailbird."

"You brightened up right before you started on Bennett's bozo. I assume you have something up your sleeve."

"Could be," I replied with a smile.

A HALF-HOUR LATER, THE PARTIES RETURNED to the deposition room, and I resumed my examination of Bruce Malone. For the first forty-five minutes I continued with my patient game plan. The I started on a new tack. "By the way, Mr. Malone, I notice from your resume that you used to be the vice-president of your profession's national organization."

"That's right."

"How come you never made it to president?"

"I quit the organization."

"Quit, or were you asked to resign?"

"I had a disagreement with the power structure."

"Didn't they ask for your resignation because you had been indicted for fraud?"

"That's what they claimed."

"And were you indicted for fraud?"

The big man's face reddened. "Yeah, but I didn't do any jail time."

"But you were convicted of fraud?"

"Well, I copped a plea."

"To fraud?"

Malone nodded.

"Did that nod mean 'yes'?"

"Yes," he replied with a sigh.

Leaving the deposition room, I was grateful that the battle of experts had come out a near draw.

CHAPTER FIFTEEN

A FEW DAYS LATER, ALGERNON WAS summoned into his immediate boss's office. He'd always had a good relationship with Matthew Bowen, the partner in charge of the trusts and estates department. Nearing retirement, Matt was a fine lawyer and a good guy. He'd been mentoring Algernon to become a partner and succeed him in running the estates department.

"Pull up a cup of coffee and grab a chair, Al." Bowen was seated behind a seven-by-three foot desk which was directly in front of the two windows reserved for non-senior partners.

Algernon poured coffee into a plain paper cup from the stand in the far corner of the room, added non-dairy creamer and sweetener, and took a seat. "What's up?"

"Our good friend Jerry has been busting my butt about McGrath."

"I guess that's because the Cardinal is busting his," Algernon replied after taking a sip. He was much more comfortable in this room, without the fancy china cups and sticky buns.

"So? Where do we stand? Jerry is pushing me to take over the case, and that won't do your partnership any good."

"It's a problem estate. The case is near trial, and our side isn't in good shape."

"What happened?"

"The lawyer representing the niece just called me. They had the examination of the handwriting experts, and our guy turned out to be a jailbird."

"Then we have a real loser."

"It's not quite that bad. The expert for the other side has a criminal record too but no jail time."

"Can we get a new expert?"

"I don't know. The court has locked both sides into their current experts. Trial's only a few weeks away, and these were the ones each side disclosed."

"Seems to me that the other side will stipulate to new experts all around."

"I'll push for it too, but I'm not sure it'll help. The present will smells like a forgery."

"Then you'd better dig up a super expert who tells it our way. The Cardinal wouldn't like it if we lost."

"WHAT THE HELL IS THIS SHIT, CAROL?" Hal McGrath demanded.

"The lamb chops that you asked for," she replied from the other end of the twelve-foot dining room table.

"What's all this bone and fat?"

"They're *shoulder* chops."

"Why don't you buy the ones you usually get—the ones I like?"

"Loin chops are *so* expensive, and these are just as good."

"Like hell they are," he groused, staring at her. "What do I give you household money for?"

She cringed, then gritted her teeth. "That's just the trouble. You only gave me half the usual this week."

He blushed slightly. "I—uh, I was a little short. Some expenses came up. I'll try to make it up in the next few weeks."

"Another 'investment'?"

He scowled at her. "Not that it's any of your business, but I may have to spring for another handwriting expert for my brother's estate."

"What's the matter with the one you have? I though he said the will was a forgery."

"He did," Hal replied, rising from the table and pushing back the plate of chops.

"Where are you going?"

"To Scully's. I can't eat this shit."

"What about your dinner?"

"I'll have something there."

". . .I thought we were low on cash."

"We are, but don't worry. I'll take it out of your next week's allowance," he concluded as he left.

AT 6:00 P.M. A FEW DAYS LATER, I stuck my head into the boss's kingdom. "Got a few minutes?"

"Sure thing, kid. Pull up a chair." Rooney was leafing through a massive file.

As I seated myself, he pushed forward an open five-pound can of salted peanuts that he had been gobbling from as he worked. "Have some. It'll put some meat on your bones."

"No, thanks. Helen's been needling me about having too much meat already."

"Yeah. Kathy's been on *my* ass for that. Been trying to put me on a diet Fortunately, she doesn't see me here. What's on your mind, McGrath?"

I nodded.

"Trial's coming up pretty soon."

"Two and a half weeks, unless it goes over because of

the experts. That's what I wanted to talk to you about."

"I hear you got a new expert from that fancy law firm," Rooney said as he stuffed another handful of peanuts into his mouth.

"Yeah, I just got his report. His credentials look great."

"He's got to be better than the ex-con you had before."

"Should be. The Cardinal's practically vouching for him."

"So what's the trouble?"

"*That's* the trouble. I don't believe the will. Why would that bitch have hired a crook if the will wasn't phony?"

Rooney shook his head. "So?"

"Mark, I don't want to put forward a forged will."

Rooney chuckled. "What choice do you have? The judge won't let us out of the case.?"

"I was talking to Herb Crowley. His uncle has this expert. He's willing to take a look at the will and some exemplars, and give me an honest opinion."

Rooney glared at me. "Are you out of your fucking *mind*?"

"Look, if it's the money, I'll pay for it out of my pocket. He'll give me a good rate."

"It's not the *money*. Don't you realize what would happen if he gave you an opinion that the will was a *forgery*?" He sighed after glancing at me. "Ian, this guy could put you between a rock and a hard place. If he says it's a forgery and you put your expert on, you might go to jail for sub-orning perjury. And if you *don't* put him on, you've set us up for a *hell* of a malpractice case. What you want to do is worse than asking a criminal client if he did it."

When I left the boss's office ten minutes later, I was even more depressed than when I'd come.

"That was simply great, Mom," I said as I pushed myself away from the table that Friday evening. "You sure know how to cook chicken."

"And you sure know how to eat it!" Helen remarked. "I thought *I* was the one who was eating for two."

"Expectant fathers have to keep up their strength, too," Sam added.

The Anjou chicken saute with onions, shallots, wine, mushrooms, and heavy cream had been divine. After apple pie with cherry vanilla ice cream, we retired to the living room for coffee. As usual, only Sam had an after-dinner brandy.

"How's things in the legal world?" he asked me.

"Very frustrating."

"Big estate case still driving you crazy?"

I nodded.

"Tell us about it," said Molly as she brought in coffee refills in a thermal carafe. "Your big case is the only excite-ment I get around here."

"What about our exciting accounting practice?" quipped Eric.

Molly shrugged and Betty glared at him.

I explained about the witness depositions and my jail-bird expert.

"Sounds pretty bad," Sam said.

"Then things got better for a while. The lawyer from the church got me a new expert, and the other side stipulated for all of us to use new experts."

"Problem solved," Helen remarked. "You even got Bennett to agree to something."

"He had to. His expert isn't any more kosher than mine. I thought we had the problem solved until today."

"Don't keep us in suspense," Sam said.

"I got a call from the chief law assistant. He directed me and Bennett to come in for a conference today to 'iron out some details.' When we got there he was very apologetic. He told us the judge wouldn't allow us to change experts. It's too near to trial, and he won't let us delay the case."

"Well," Sam sighed, "at least it's even."

CHAPTER SIXTEEN

FOR THE NEXT TWO WEEKS, I WORKED feverishly on the case. I boned up on the rules of evidence and prepared memoranda on potential legal issues. I had several meetings with Alice and the two witnesses; at my insistence, one was even held at my office during business hours. Since I'd been forced to use Gambi, I met with my jailbird expert twice. I persuaded the man to wear a conservative suit for the trial and discussed with him how we were going to take the sting out of his criminal conviction. "Look, Mario—when I ask you if you've ever been convicted of a crime, I want you to admit it freely. You will tell the jury that you were wrong, you've learned your lesson, and you'll never do something like that again." Gambi assured me of his contrition. I worked closely with Algernon Flynn too, and received considerable help from the church attorney's firm. When we made our deal, Flynn had promised to earn his client's piece of the action, and he appeared to be living up to it.

On the day of the trial I met Alice in the courtroom—amazingly, on time. Bennett had both Hal and Charlie wearing dark, conservative suits. Flynn was in court but had no one with him. Shortly after nine-thirty, the court officer banged his gavel and announced, "All rise. The Surrogate's Court of the State of New York, County of Westchester, is now in session. Honorable Albert Carter presiding."

Judge Carter strode into the courtroom with a first-thing-in-the-morning-smile painted on his lips. "Good morning, ladies and gentlemen."

"Good morning, Your Honor," the Greek chorus replied.

"Mr. Casey, please call the calendar."

The court officer rose from his seat at a desk to the left judge's bench. Because of his excessive weight, standing up was a great effort, and the brass buttons on his uniform coat seemed ready to pop. He studied the sheet of paper in front of him and finally announced, "Probate proceeding, Estate of James McGrath."

Bennett and I each answered ready.

"Gentlemen," said the judge, "under the rules, I am required to hold a settlement conference immediately prior to the selection of the jury. Will counsel please join me in my robing room?"

He left the bench and went through the door immediately behind; we were required to take the long way around. The judge motioned us to seats. He was behind his desk, puffing on a small cigar. "The smoking lamp is lit, gentlemen."

Neither I nor Bennett were smokers, but Flynn lit a Marlboro.

"Now, let's see whether we can resolve this matter without bringing in a jury." The judge looked down at the file, then up at Flynn. "This conference is for lawyers. What are you doing here?"

"I'm sorry, Your Honor," I said. "I should have introduced my colleague. This is Algernon Flynn, of the firm of Duffy, Donovan and Scala. He's my co-counsel."

"That's a fine firm, Mr. Flynn. How did you get into this matter?"

The young man put on a shy smile. He was in his element. "As you know, Your Honor, my firm represents the archdiocese. One of Mr. McGrath's nieces is a nun at the Convent of the Sacred Heart in Houston. He had promised to leave all, or much, of his estate to the convent, which is in sad need of repair. The sister and her family believe there is a later will that fulfills this promise. We haven't been able to locate it yet. The family believes that the decedent also may have wanted to benefit his niece, Alice Keller, who had been assisting him in his business for several years, and for that reason the convent agreed to cooperate with Ms. Keller under an arrangement where both would benefit no matter which will was finally probated. The cardinal has asked my firm to assist the convent in this connection."

"That sounds like a noble endeavor," said the judge, smiling broadly. "Since the church is involved, wouldn't it be more seemly if this matter could be resolved without what promises to be a nasty trial?" he continued, glaring at Bennett.

"I'm sure that the convent wouldn't be averse to leaving something to the decedent's siblings," Flynn replied in his most syrupy tone. "Christian charity would certainly dictate that."

"And is the petitioner willing to compromise, Mr. Elkins?"

"I'll speak to my client."

"And your objectants, Mr. Bennett? Are they willing to be reasonable?"

Joe Bennett felt extremely uncomfortable. He had promised Hal too much, or at least implied it. He had to tread lightly. "My clients are very reasonable people. I'll speak to them."

"Why don't both of you gentlemen speak to your respective clients, then report back to me." As we all got up, Carter motioned for Flynn to remain. "How long have you been with the firm?"

"Over seven years."

"You a partner?"

"Not yet, but maybe this year."

"Jerry Donovan still with the firm?"

"Yes, sir, he's the managing partner."

"Send him my regards. We were at Fordham Law together."

"I sure will."

"I'll bet he's the one with connections to the archdiocese. He was always bragging about his church contacts."

"You hit it on the nose, judge. He was a boyhood friend of the cardinal."

For the next ten minutes the judge bored Algernon with war stories of his youth, exploits, and importance while the young lawyer worked hard to appear interested and impressed. There came a knock on the door, and Bennett and I returned to the robing room. Neither of us was smiling.

"So how did it go?" the judge asked. "Can we settle?"

"I don't think so, Judge," Bennett replied. "My client insists that it's a forged will, and that Ms. Keller should be satisfied with her one-fourth share under intestacy. The best we can do is to waive any claim for legals and penalties for her misconduct."

Judge Carter shook his head and turned to Ian. "What about your client, Mr. Elkins?"

I grimaced. "I don't think I can do much better, Judge. My client says that the will's perfectly good and that her uncles should know it. She's already given away a big chunk to the church, and she really wants to have something left for herself. Of course she will waive sanctions for frivolous objections if Mr. Bennett's clients drop the case now."

The judge frowned, then ground out his cigar in a glass ashtray on his desk. "I don't think either of you has tried hard enough. I guess I'd better speak to the parties directly."

"Do you want them sent in together or one at a time?" Bennett inquired.

"No, we'll do it together in open court."

A few minutes later we were all seated at the counsel tables when the judge returned to the courtroom to John Casey's booming, "All rise."

"Be seated," he said as he ascended the bench. "Lady and gentlemen, this case should be settled. If it goes to the jury, the loser could be very badly hurt." Both Alice and the McGrath brothers looked strangely at him, and he chuckled. "You're wondering how the loser can be hurt. Let me educate you. The main defense to the probate of this will is the claim that it's a forgery. If the jury finds that to be the fact, Ms.—" he looked down at the file— "Keller will find herself civilly, or even criminally, embarrassed. At the very least I will sanction her for the reasonable legal fees of the objectants, and I might well report it to the district attorney for possible prosecution."

Alice struggled mightily to maintain a blank expression.

"And," the judge continued, "if the jury finds the will valid, I may very well determine to sanction the objectants for frivolous objections, which will mean that, instead of getting a share of this large estate, they will not only have to pay their own legal expense but be ordered to reimburse the estate for all the legal expense their objections caused .... On the other hand, if you people are reasonable, all of you will walk out of this court with something in your purse or pockets."

"Does Your Honor have any suggestions on how this case could be settled?" I asked.

The judge smiled broadly. "I'm glad you asked, Mr. Elkins."

In the first place, all legals should come off the top of the estate. That would include your firm's legals, Mr. Flynn."

"What about the fees we've already paid?" Hal and Alice asked in unison.

"I'm coming to that. All fees will be fixed by me based on my evaluation of an affidavit of services from each attorney, and each party who has paid legal fees will be reimbursed by the estate. Now as to the shares of Messrs. Mc-Grath, each of you would be entitled to one-quarter of the estate if there is no will, or nothing if there is one. If each of you gets one-eighth, you should be satisfied."

"What about the share of Mrs. Curran?" I asked.

The judge looked puzzled.

"That's the decedent's sister, Your Honor," I said.

The judge nodded. "The nun's mother. Is she represented?"

"No, Your Honor," Flynn replied.

"I assume her share will go to the convent."

"I don't think so, judge," said Flynn. "Sister Mary Elizabeth has insisted that her mother keep hers. I assume that, after Mrs. Curran dies, the balance will go to the convent, but not before."

"In any event," the judge continued, "she would get an eighth, and if we settle we'll need her consent. That leaves five-eighths, which could go three-eighths to Ms. Keller and a quarter to the convent. . . . Well, what do you say?"

"Sounds good to me, judge," replied Flynn. "Of course, I'll have to check with the client."

The judge nodded. "And you, Ms. Keller?"

"I'd like a little time to think about it," she answered with a troubled expression.

"Don't bother," boomed Hal. "It doesn't please me one bit. I'm not giving away half my inheritance to that—"

Joe Bennett shook him before he could complete his remark.

"Okay, lady and gentlemen," the judge concluded. "Let's bring in the jury.   Mr. Casey, send down for the panel."

CHAPTER SEVENTEEN

WHEN ALGERNON FLYNN RETURNED to his office after juror selection, he found a message from Donovan, who wanted to see him as soon as possible. He had his secretary call and was told to come right over. When he entered Donovan's domain, the managing partner was seated behind his desk, sipping scotch from a lowboy glass half-filled with ice. "Take a load off," he said, pointing to a visitor's chair. "Has the trial started yet?"

"We've just finished selecting jurors. Opening statements are scheduled for tomorrow afternoon."

"The cardinal called me today." Donovan emptied his glass and refilled it from a square bottle next to his left hand. "He was wondering how the trial's going. What shall I tell him?"

The young man's mouth watered slightly. He sorely wanted to be offered a drink, but it didn't seem to be in the offing. "It's too early to tell, sir."

Donovan reached into an ice bucket and dropped two cubes into his glass. "Oh, I realize that, but I believe that what he really wants is to be assured of the ultimate result."

Flynn coughed. His throat was dry. "I don't know what to say, sir. It's far too early. The jurors we selected seem okay, but our handwriting expert is a convicted felon."

Donovan used a tissue to wipe a few drops of moisture from the leather panel on the top of his desk. "Didn't you tell me that there was a later will leaving all or a substantial amount to the convent?"

Flynn eyed the drink. "That's what the decedent's sister thinks, but we haven't had any luck finding it. That's why we made the deal with the niece."

"Thelma," said Donovan, speaking into the intercom, "could you please bring me a bowl of pretzels?" The partner sipped his drink until the pretzels arrived, then nibbled on a few. "Good scotch always tastes better with something salty."

The young man nodded.

"It would be wonderful if that new will turned up. The

cardinal would be very pleased."

"Yes, sir,"

"And," the managing partner continued, "the cardinal has done many good things for us. An associate who is able to please our benefactor can go far in this firm."

"Yes, sir."

" I won't keep you from your work. Just keep me informed."

The young man's shirt was drenched when he left.

Five minutes later, the intercom in Matt Bowen's office buzzed. "Yes, Grace."

"It's Mr. Donovan."

". . .Hi, Jerry. To what do I owe the pleasure of this call?"

"Have you ever tasted twenty-five-year-old Macallan?"

"That's too rich for my pocketbook. With two kids in college, I can barely afford the twelve-year-old."

"There's a glass, an ice bucket, and a bottle of it on my desk just waiting for you."

"Be right over."

Three minutes went by before Matt Bowen was seated in the chair recently vacated by his young associate, and sipping scotch. "Well, what do you think?" the managing partner asked.

"Nectar of the gods. If only *I'd* gone to school with a cardinal."

They sipped their drinks for a while before Donovan brought up the real reason for their meeting. "I had young Flynn in a few minutes ago."

"He's a bright young man. He'd make a good partner."

"Perhaps, but right now I have bigger fish to fry."

"McGrath?"

Donovan nodded as he munched on a three-ring pretzel. He pushed the bowl over to Bowen, who shook his head. Unlike good scotch, pretzels were wasted calories.

"I was asking him about the probable results of the trial. He was noncommittal but pessimistic."

"I didn't know he was back from court. Where does the trial stand?"

"They've selected jurors."

"Then he's right—too early to tell."

"And the pessimism?"

"You know about the jailbird handwriting expert?"

"The other side's expert isn't much cleaner, but that's not really the issue. We need a backup plan. I suggested the later will, but he tells me they haven't located it."

"We have an investigator working on that, but these things take time, and even assuming we find it, who can predict what it will say?"

"That's why we need a more effective and more selective search."

Bowen eyed his senior partner with a knowing look.

"You know how much the cardinal wants to help his brother from Texas?"

"Yeah."

"And how happy it would make him if we succeeded in finding a new will that goes all or mostly all our way."

Bowen nodded.

"Well, I impressed on him how important it would be to his partnership chances if such a will were found."

"Jerry, that's awfully heavy pressure on him. With his whole career at stake, he's likely to do something desperate or even illegal."

"So? It's for the greater good."

"If it's that important, maybe I ought to take over and use my contacts."

Donovan shook his head. "No, Matt. It would look terrible for this firm if a partner were disbarred or, even worse, sent to prison. Just add to the pressure,and make sure he has access to your resources."

"I'll do it, but I don't like it."

"What's the matter, Matt?"

"Law is an ethical profession."

"Think of it as striving for the greater good. That convent deserves the money a lot more than the McGrath family."

"I'll call him in now. Did you leave him sober enough to talk to?"

Donovan chuckled. "Be serious. Do you think I'd waste twenty-five-year-old Macallan's on an *associate?*"

AN HOUR LATER, ALGERNON FLYNN left Matt Bowen's office. He was hyped from the pep talk but calmed by virtue of two tumblers of Cutty Sark. Back in his room, he punched his auto-dialer. "Mr. Lutz, please. . . . Tell him it's Mr. Flynn. . . . Hey, Sally, how're you doing? . . . Great, how's crime these days? . . . You have time for me to buy you a drink and pick your brain? . . . Seven-thirty at O'Neil's'll be fine."

Sal Lutz had been one of Flynn's closest friends at law school. They'd drunk, studied, chased women together, and were about even in class standing. Sal's uncle Vito had a lucrative criminal practice and had taken his nephew into the firm. The two young men had remained close and frequently consulted each other. The price was always a few rounds of drinks.

O'Neil's was a quiet pub on thirty-seventh off Madison. The drinks were substantial and not overpriced. As to the food, the grilled American cheese wouldn't kill you. Flynn got there at 7:25 and saw Lutz seated at the fifteen-foot bar. There were three other men drinking but only one of the six tables along the side, which ran the depth of the store, was occupied. Algernon patted him on the back and, turning to the bartender, said, "Kevin, my friend and I will be moving to your back table. Please bring a double refill for him and a double Cutty on the rocks for me. We'll be running a tab that goes to me."

"Sure thing, Mr. Flynn," replied the bartender, scratching his red-bristled mustache.

"Playing any squash lately?" Flynn asked when the two were seated.

"I haven't had the time, Al."

"You should really make some. Exercise is good for your health and figure."

"Try telling Uncle Vito that—and you're right, I must have put on twenty pounds in the last year, but these crumbs we represent are constantly feeding us, and you can't say no. I'm going to have to buy some new suits," Lutz concluded, looking down at a stylish double-breasted glen plaid that was pulling at the buttons.

"My firm has a membership in a squash and health club. You can be my guest any time you want."

"I'll try to take you up on that, but call me and give me a nudge next time you go."

". . .So tell me, Sally—how is crime these days?" asked Flynn, taking a sip of his scotch.

"It's a boom business. Keeps us occupied and well paid. Which area are you interested in? Need someone to help you guys steal from your estates?"

Flynn chuckled. "Great idea. I'll keep it in mind. No,

I'm looking for a different specialty today."

"Name it. We've got a huge inventory of crooks."

"Ever represent any good forgers?"

Lutz smiled. "You're in luck. Uncle Vito and I just finished a forgery trial. The client's a very talented guy."

"Is he on the loose?"

"Yeah, the jury was very kind to us."

"Could I meet the guy?"

"Sure thing. What for?"

"I'm in a will probate trial, and the other side claims the will was a forgery. I'd like to get an education in the forgery business."

THE DELAY IN THE START OF THE TRIAL caused other scheduling changes. I returned to my office and was able to get most of my work done, allowing me to get home at six, at least an hour earlier than usual. When I reached the apartment I ran into Molly at the door. "Hi, Mom. How are you?"

"Not too bad, Ian," she replied, giving me a peck. "I wish I could say as much for Helen."

"What's the matter? She looked fine when I left this morning."

"You men are all the same. You never notice anything. She's pregnant, you know."

"Is she alright?"

"Well, she's not *sick* or anything, but she's very close to delivering and very delicate."

"Is she having labor pains?"

"Probably not, but soon. Just open your eyes and look," Molly concluded and marched out the door.

In the kitchen, I found Helen stirring a pot on the stove. "Are you okay?" I asked, failing to completely hide my hysteria.

"I'm fine," she replied, as she kissed me. "Why do you ask?"

I explained.

She laughed. "You know my mother's a worry wort. Sure I'm close, but I'm not there yet."

"Well, what did she mean?"

She shook her head. "Make yourself a drink, get me a club soda, and we'll sit down and I'll tell you about it."

I poured myself a white wine and set the drinks on the living room cocktail table. "So?" I asked. "You know I took a half personal day so that Mom and I could shop for some baby things."

I nodded.

"When we were in the store, I got a cramp and had to go to the ladies room."

"Is that all?"

She shrugged. "I got another one after we got home."

"Isn't that a sign of labor?"

"Could be. Could also be Braxton-Hicks."

"What's that?"

"Don't you lawyers know anything outside of the law? It's false labor."

"So shouldn't you call the doctor?"

She shook her head. "Don't be silly. I know when I have to call."

"Uh—"

"When the pains come regularly at least every ten minutes. Twice in an afternoon, even if they *are* labor pains, is much too early."

"What if they start coming every ten minutes while you're in the office? Maybe you ought to start your maternity leave now."

She laughed. "Look, Ian, stop being an old lady. That's my mother's job. If I get regular labor pains when I'm in the office, I call a cab and go to the hospital. I'd go out of my mind if I had to stay home and wait for the baby. Now promise me you'll stop worrying."

I did but remained concerned. What if the baby came in the next few days, during the trial?

CHAPTER EIGHTEEN

A S USUAL, I GOT TO COURT FAR TOO EARLY. I had to wait over half an hour before the courtroom was unlocked. When the calendar was called thirty minutes later I learned that Bennett was locked in a massive traffic jam caused by a jackknifed truck, and that the trial had been adjourned to the following morning.

As I repacked my bag, Alice glared at me. "Why do I have to waste my time here? I have a lot of work to do."

I shrugged. "What do you want from me? I didn't cause the accident, and I'm stuck here, too. I'll see you here at nine-thirty, and bring the witnesses. I assume we'll put them on after opening statements."

"See you tomorrow, Ian," said Flynn on his way to the door.

"See you, Al."

The minute Flynn left the courtroom, he punched a number into his cell phone. "Hello, Max. . . . It's Al Flynn. I'm out of court early. Can I come over now? . . . Great. See you."

BY 5:30 FLYNN HAD RETURNED TO THE OFFICE. He went directly to the desk of his boss's secretary. "Nora, is Mr. Bowen available?"

"I'll check, Mr. Flynn," replied the thin, dark-haired woman, in her late forties who'd been Matt Bowen's secretary ever since he became a partner. ". . .You can go right in," she said, hanging up the intercom.

"Hi, Matt," the young man said as he seated himself.

"How did the openings go?" Bowen asked, looking up from a pile of papers.

"They didn't. Joe Bennett got stuck in traffic, and the judge adjourned the trial till tomorrow."

"Where've you been?"

"That's what I wanted to talk to you about. I was introduced to a guy who has a special talent for turning up missing wills."

"Who is he?"

Flynn blushed slightly. "I can't tell you. It was one of

the conditions of the intro."

Bowen eyed him strangely.

"I'm told the guy's not too kosher, but he's reliable."

"What's he cost?"

"He's expensive."

". . . How expensive?"

"Twelve thousand."

". . .That's a lot of dough for a pig in a poke."

"We're not at risk unless he produces—that is, except for the front money."

"How much is that?"

"Twenty-five hundred."

Bowen let out air. "I'll have to talk to Jerry."

"I need to know right away."

"You will. I'll talk to him now. How should the check read?"

Flynn shook his head. "Gotta be cash."

Five minutes later, Bowen was seated in front of Jerry Donovan's desk. "So what do we do?" he asked.

"What choice do we have?"

Bowen shrugged. "Do we *have* that much in cash?"

Donovan snorted. "In the safe. I'll have to tell Neil," he added, referring to the chairman of the executive committee. "Don't look so grim. I know you don't have the stomach for this, but sometimes we have to. I'll bring the money to you shortly. You were right about that young man. He's very enterprising. If he survives this, he'll make a useful partner."

WHEN MARY CURRAN GOT HOME from work that evening in Houston, she noticed the light on her answering machine was flashing. It'll keep, she thought as she first washed up, then made herself a vodka and tonic. With two of those she could face anything. She punched the play button. There were three messages. The first was a charitable solicitation, the second a computerized sales pitch to cover her house with aluminum siding. She immediately deleted both. The third message, less than an hour old, had come from a lawyer named Jason Kelly about her brother's estate. Sister Mary Elizabeth had told him to call her, and could she please call him this evening, as he would be working late.

When she returned the call, she learned that his firm represented the archdiocese. Her daughter was facing a serious legal and ethical problem relating to the estate, it had to be dealt with immediately, and it would be better to speak in person rather than over the phone. "Would it be possible for me to come to your home this evening?"

"Not meaning any disrespect, Mr. Kelly, but how do I know who you are?"

"You're absolutely right, Mrs. Curran. If you will hold for a few minutes, I'll try to patch your daughter into this call."

Mary Elizabeth joined in and confirmed who Kelly was. She had gotten permission from the mother superior to come home that evening, she explained, and Mr. Kelly was picking her up on the way.

IT WAS 9:00 WHEN THE TWO ARRIVED. Mary Elizabeth was in her full habit, the first time she had worn it home. Mary remembered seeing her right after she took her final vows. She was a little shocked at the gray, slightly informal outfit. When she was growing up nuns, like penguins, were strictly in black and white. Kelly was a young man not quite thirty, with curly brown hair, wearing a raincoat over a gray herringbone suit. Mary ushered them into the living room and offered coffee and cookies. They accepted only the coffee. She poured and left the vacuum carafe on the cocktail table. After a few minutes' silence, she finally asked, "So what's this all about?"

"I think it would be best to tell it in sequence," Kelly began. "You received the call from Mr. Flynn, Sister."

Mary Elizabeth took a sip of her coffee. "Yes. Yesterday. He told me the trial was beginning, and that Cousin Alice and he had made a deal that there would be a split between the convent and her no matter which will was finally admitted. He asked me to come to New York—practically ordered me to. What an arrogant young man he is. He wanted me to testify to how much Uncle Jim loved Alice and how he couldn't stand Hal and Charlie."

"I guess he believes that having a nun, wearing a full habit and offering such testimony, would show the jury that God is on Alice's side," Kelly added.

"That's probably why he didn't ask *me*," said Mary. She was pleased with her daughter's spunk, but wondered if she wasn't too assertive for a nun. Maybe she should have married. That way she'd have a husband to boss around. "What're you going to do?" Mary asked.

"That's what we're here for," Mary Elizabeth replied. "In any event, I first spoke to Mother Superior. She asked me what I could truthfully testify to. I told her that, while I was sure Uncle Jim was down on Hal and Charlie—especially Charlie—I wasn't so sure how he felt about Alice. She put me in touch with the archdiocese's lawyers, and I ended up speaking to Mr. Kelly."

"I don't much like Mr. Flynn," Mary commented.

"Neither do I," Kelly assured her, "and I went to law school with him. In fact we were moot court partners. Al's a slippery sort of a guy—very smooth, but I always feel I've got to count my fingers after we shake hands."

"Frankly," said Mary, "I don't understand why the convent made a deal with Alice. I'm *sure* there's another will that leaves everything to it."

"But we haven't been able to find it yet, and you haven't a clue to which lawyer drew the will. At least this way the convent gets something."

The older woman shrugged. "If the will fails, I get a quarter of the estate, and I can give that to the convent."

"You will *not*!" Mary Elizabeth snapped. "You'll need that money for your retirement. If there's anything left, you can leave it in your will."

"In the first place, young lady, it will be *my* property to do with as I please. Anyway, what's the difference if I give it or if it goes to the convent through the deal you're talking about?"

The young nun blushed. "None, but at least you won't be *giving* it away."

"Ladies, may we please get back to the issue at hand? Should Sister Mary Elizabeth testify?"

"What do you think?" Mary asked.

"Well, in the first place, I'd be surprised if the judge let that kind of testimony in, but assuming he did, and as long as Sister Mary Elizabeth tells the absolute truth, it can't do any harm."

"What would I say?"

"That your Uncle Jim was very unfriendly to your Uncles Hal and Charlie, and that, in fact, he fired Charlie."

"What about Cousin Alice?"

"You don't know how he felt about her, but he must have felt something since he had her working for him."

On this there was general agreement.

CHAPTER NINETEEN

THE FOLLOWING MORNING, EVERYONE was in court on time. Surprisingly, I was not the first to arrive. When the case was answered ready, the judge called the lawyers into his robing room. After we were seated, he looked slowly around the room. "Gentlemen, we will have opening statements this morning, followed by one or two of petitioner's witnesses. I have several matters on this afternoon, so, at the lunch hour, we will adjourn until tomorrow morning."

Excuse me, Your Honor, but will that be the procedure throughout the trial?" Bennett asked. "I need to know so I can plan my witness scheduling."

"No. Most days we will do a full day. With respect to

the opening statements," the judge continued, fixing his eyes on Bennett, "I want it understood that they will be given in a proper and respectful manner. There will be no outrageous or nasty accusations, and if there are, a lawyer may well find himself sleeping behind bars. Do I make myself clear?"

We all said he had.

"Is Your Honor directing me not to advise the jury that I have a good faith belief that Mr. Elkins was involved in forging the alleged will?" asked Bennett.

The judge shook his head dejectedly. "Mr. Bennett, while I believe that you are barking up the wrong tree and can't possibly prove that absurd allegation, I will not prevent or punish you for stating it to the jury. However, I *will* instruct the jury that anything the lawyers say is not evidence, and I will specifically refer to any statement you make accusing Mr. Elkins of anything to do with a claimed forgery. Furthermore, in the event that you don't offer at least some credible and admissible evidence on that issue, I will sanction you for contempt. Additionally, I will instruct the jury again that what you said is not evidence and that you have not offered them any evidence to prove the accusation. If I have to do that, I don't believe the jury will look too favorably on your clients' position. Are you clear on that point?"

"Yes, Your Honor."

"Well, then, I sincerely hope you won't be foolish enough to test me on it. Okay, gentlemen, let's go out and give your openings."

When we returned to the courtroom the judge instructed the clerk to bring in the jury. After the five men and three women had taken their seats, he addressed them. Most important, he told them, was not to discuss the case with anyone, including their families, and not to form any opinions until all the evidence was in and they were sent out to deliberate. He then explained opening statements, nodded to me and reclined in his high-backed chair.

I STEPPED UP TO A PODIUM in front of the jury box, bringing a single sheet of yellow legal paper that I placed on the stand. "Thank you, Your Honor. Ladies and gentlemen, as his honor has told you, my name is Ian Elkins, and I represent Alice Keller, who was named executrix in a document we will prove is the last will and testament of James McGrath. The will was not done by a lawyer. It was typed on a printed form by Ms Keller, Mr. McGrath's niece and employee. Alice will testify that her uncle came to her house for her sister's birthday party and brought the forms with him. He asked her to type the will, told her what he wanted, and she typed exactly what he told her to. Then he signed the will, which was witnessed by two family friends who were guests at the party. Mr. McGrath's brothers, Harold and Charles, are objecting to the will. Both of them were on bad terms with their brother James. If there is no valid will, they will share in their brother's estate."

My opening was interrupted by the coughing of one of the jurors. The elderly woman sitting next to him gave him a cough drop. That seemed to work, and when it was quiet, I continued.

"The McGrath brothers claim the will is a forgery, and they have hired an expert witness to testify that the signature on it does not compare favorably with exemplars of Mr. McGrath's writing. Ms. Keller has also engaged an expert, who will testify that a comparison of the signature on the will with samples of James McGrath's writing show that the will is genuine. Because of procedural standards in cases like this, the handwriting witness for the objectants will testify first, and Alice Keller's expert with testify in what is called rebuttal. I should also inform you that both handwriting experts have previously had problems with the criminal law. You will need to listen to each of them carefully and determine which one you will believe. Having spoken to each of you during the jury selection phase of this trial, I'm sure you will listen to all of the evidence with an open mind and make a fair and honest decision. Now I assume Mr. Bennett will want to tell you about his case."

As I seated myself the judge turned to Bennett, who rose from his seat and faced the jury. "Thank you, Mr. Elkins, but I will reserve my opening remarks until after you put your witnesses on. That way the jury will have a more organized picture of my clients' objections."

The judge turned towards me. "Okay, Mr. Elkins. Call your first witness."

I called Jack Gorman, whose testimony was substantially identical to his deposition. On cross Bennett hammered at him but got nowhere. He went on about Gorman's closeness to the family, and that he was engaged to Alice's sister. Over my strong objections, he demanded to know how much he was being paid to lie, but the effort fell flat. Between objections and side bar rulings, he wasted nearly an hour on Jack.

After Gorman left the stand, the judge called a ten-minute recess that lasted half an hour. When the court was called to order, I announced, "Petitioner calls Lester Smith."

As Smith sauntered up to the witness stand, the intercom on the judge's bench rang. He picked up the phone and spoke for several minutes. Then he announced, "An emergency has come up. We will have to end this session earlier than I expected. This matter is adjourned until tomorrow morning at 10:30. Please be on time."

When the judge left the bench, Smith strode up to Alice. "What is this crap? I'm here to testify today. I'm not coming back tomorrow!"

"But, Les, you've *got* to."

He ignored her and stormed out.

"You'd better talk to him tonight," I said.

She shrugged.

"Alice, there's no choice. We need the testimony of *two* subscribing witnesses in order to make a *prima facie* case. Otherwise the judge will have to throw us out."

"I'll do what I can," she concluded, and left.

As I left the courtroom, I called my office on my cell. "Hi, Rosie, I'm leaving court now. I'll be in the office in an hour."

"Not if you want to live."

"What's up?"

"Your mother-in-law just called. Your wife took a taxi to the hospital. She wants to know where the hell you are."

"If she calls again, tell her I'm on my way."

I got my car and raced to the Bronx. Fortunately the Cross-Westchester wasn't jammed up. Less than an hour later I was at Montefiore Hospital and parked in their over-priced garage. Sam was sitting in an armchair in the maternity waiting room, reading a file.

"How is she?"

"She's in the labor room with Mom. Men aren't welcome, I'm told. Have a seat. Waiting's the papa's job."

"That's nonsense. Husbands have been allowed in labor rooms for years.

"That's hospital rules. This comes from your wife and

mother-in-law."

I complied, and an hour later Molly stomped in. "You finally got here!" she growled.

"Don't pick on the poor boy. He's been with me over an hour."

"What took him so long? I called his office at ten-thirty."

"I'm sorry, Mom, I was in court. How is she?"

"You men are all the same. No sense of priority."

"How *is* she?" Sam asked with a shrug.

"She's fine. The doctor says she thinks it's false labor. If nothing happens in the next hour, she can go home—and, by the way, she's been moved to a regular room, and you can visit her."

Five minutes later, Helen had three visitors. She was alone, in the window bed of a two-patient room. "I feel stupid dragging everybody here on a false alarm."

"Do it as many times as it takes," I replied, kissing her. "Just so long as the two of you are okay," I patted her belly.

"Hey, none of that monkey business," Sam joshed. "That's my daughter."

"And you never patted her when she was on the inside?" Molly asked.

WE CONTINUED BANTERING for the next hour and a half, at which time the obstetrician examined Helen and signed her out. Within the hour, she had been wheeled to the entrance of the hospital, and I drove her home.

Over her objections that she was feeling fine and perfectly able to cook dinner, I ordered in from a local Chinese restaurant: wonton soup, boneless spareribs with hot mustard and duck sauce, and beef with broccoli in a brown sauce. We sat down afterward in the living room for tea. "That was good," she said. "I like being spoiled."

"So why don't you take the next few days off from work?"

She shook her head. "Mother's right. You men are all alike. I feel fine, and the doctor says the baby may not come for weeks. I'd go out of my mind staying home." As she stood up to emphasize her point, Helen suddenly grasped her stomach and sat down.

"What's the matter?" I asked.

She put a finger to her lips and looked down at her wrist watch. After a little while she flinched again. "Eight minutes, I'd better call Dr. Friedman. I think this time it's for real."

At 10:45 that evening Carol Rachel Elkins, named after her parents' maternal grandmothers, was born. She tipped the scales at seven pounds five ounces. On hearing the news, I opened a box of cigars, vowing that I would even offer one to Bennett.

CHAPTER TWENTY

I WAS TIRED WHEN I REACHED the court the next morning. It had been well after midnight before he left the hospital. Molly tried to press me into sleeping late and visiting Helen when visiting hours started; Sam had set her straight about professional priorities.

I was wondering whether my second attesting witness would show up. When the calendar was called at nine-thirty, neither Alice nor Smith had appeared. "Are you gentlemen ready to proceed?" asked the judge.

"I'm waiting for my witnesses, Your Honor. They may be stuck in traffic."

"In that case I'll take care of a few conferences in my robing room. Let me know when they get here."

"Excuse me, Your Honor," I said, "but would I be out of line in offering you and counsel a cigar to celebrate the birth of my daughter last night?"

"Not at all, Mr. Elkins. Congratulations. Is she your first?"

I nodded.

"But I must warn you," the judge continued as he took the cigar, "that I'd better not catch you offering them to the jurors." He left the amid a few chuckles.

"Thanks for the cigar, Elkins. I hope you don't mind if I give it to my client."

"No problem, Joe. Why don't you take another, so each of them gets one?"

"Thanks. I hope your witnesses show."

"I'm sure they'll be here shortly," I replied with less confidence than I felt.

As if in answer to my prayer, Alice walked into the courtroom at that moment with Lester Smith in tow.

Half an hour later the judge returned to the courtroom and, on learning that everybody was present, called in the jury. Lester Smith testified as he had in his deposition. Bennett's cross-examination was much less vigorous than it had been for Jack Gorman. He stressed Smith's romantic involvement with Alice and let it go at that.

I called Alice. I had agonized over whether to do so or to wait for rebuttal. Technically, the two subscribing witnesses had made my prima facie case, but I believed that the jury might take it amiss if I held her back. I brought her through her relationship with her uncle from her initial contacts as a little girl, her employment by him as Charlie's assistant, and her promotion to manager when Charlie was fired for taking graft, culminating with Moira's birthday party, when Uncle Jim dictated the will to her. She described what had happened when Jim signed the will and Jack and Les acted as witnesses. "Did your sister, Moira, see the will being signed and witnessed?" I asked.

"Yes, she did."

"Will she be here to testify?"

"No, she died a few months later from cancer," Alice answered sadly.

At that emotional high point, I concluded my direct examination.

AFTER LUNCH, WE RE-BRIEFED ALICE on what she could expect on cross. "Your direct examination went very well," I said. "If Bennett asks the same questions he did at your depositions, he can't do you much harm, but there can be surprises. Is there anything else he can bring up that I don't know about?"

She looked at me strangely. "Absolutely not."

"Please, Alice, I'm not trying to insult you, but if there's anything I don't know, tell me now. That way we can decide how to meet it."

"Ian, I know you mean well, but there's nothing I haven't told you."

"Okay, let's go back to court and get this over with."

By 2:20 the jury was back in their box, and Bennett began. For the first twenty minutes he went over the materials he had covered in her depositions. Then he appeared to be winding up. "Ms. Keller, are you absolutely sure that your uncle James McGrath was at your apartment on October 12?"

"Yes, that's when he signed his will."

"And how was his health?"

"Not bad."

"Wasn't he having heart problems?"

"Mild ones."

"And hadn't he been hospitalized for his heart?"

"At times."

"And on October 12, 1996, wasn't he a patient at Fordham Hospital?"

"He'd been in around that time."

"And wasn't he *in* Fordham Hospital on October 12, 1996?"

"That was the Saturday the will was signed. He was at my apartment for Moira's birthday."

"Excuse me, Your Honor, but there is a subpoenaed document I'd like to retrieve."

"Check with the clerk."

A few minutes later, Bennett returned with a small folder. He pulled out a sheaf of papers and showed it to Alice.

"Objection, Your Honor!" I exclaimed. "*I* haven't seen these papers. What are they?"

"Certified business records of Fordham Hospital showing records of the hospitalization of James McGrath," Bennett replied primly.

The judge said, "have the reporter mark them for identification, then show the papers to Mr. Elkins."

Bennett complied. As I read them I had a difficult time maintaining my composure. James McGrath had been hospitalized at Fordham on October 8 and had not been discharged until October 15.

Bennett offered the record into evidence and had Alice read the appropriate portions aloud to the jury. Then he announced, "No further questions from this witness."

"Re-direct, Mr. Elkins?" the judge asked.

"May I have a few minutes' recess, Your Honor?"

The judge motioned us up to the bench. "Mr. Elkins, I can't allow you to confer with your client now."

"I fully realize that, Judge, and I won't speak to her, but I do want to confer with my colleague."

"Ten-minute recess, but Ms. Keller remains in the witness box and you will not communicate with her."

"Thank you, Your Honor."

Flynn and I left the courtroom. I asked him,"what do you think we should do?"

"No question in my mind. You've got to ask her to explain. Whatever she says can't be any worse than saying nothing."

"You're right."

When the court was called to order, I rose. "Ms. Keller, you have testified that, on October 12, your uncle, Mr. McGrath, was at your home signing his will. According to the record from Fordham Hospital, he was a patient there on that date. Can you explain?"

"Certainly," she replied with a look of complete confidence. "After I invited Uncle Jim to Moira's party, I learned that he was in the hospital, and I assumed he wouldn't be there. Then, in the late morning I got a phone call from him asking what time the party was. I said that I thought he was in the hospital, and he said he was, but that he was feeling much better and that the doctor told him it would be okay to leave unofficially, come to the party, and then return to the hospital. I offered to pick him up, but he said it wasn't necessary, that he'd take a taxi. When the party was over, I offered to drive him back, but he insisted on taking a cab back, too."

"Wasn't it unusual for a patient to be allowed to leave the hospital to go to a party and then return without being discharged?"

"*I* always thought so," she replied with a smile, "but Uncle Jim usually got his own way."

"No further questions," I said.

"Recross?" the judge asked.

Bennett sprang to his feet and strode up to her. "That was a cute story, Ms. Keller. Now how about telling us the truth?" he demanded, his nose practically touching hers.

"*Objection!*" I shouted. "He's bullying the witness. Have him ask questions, not make statements."

"So your client can continue lying, Elkins?"

"*Objection*," I repeated.

"Mr. Bennett, you will control yourself. I will not permit you to badger the witness or make statements. You will limit yourself to asking proper questions. Do you *understand?*"

"Yes, Your Honor."

"The jury will disregard Mr. Bennett's outburst. It was thoroughly improper, and nothing that he said is evidence .... Now, Mr. Bennett, do you have any thing else?"

"No, Your Honor."

"Call your next witness, Mr. Elkins."

I was about to announce that the petitioner would rest when Algernon Flynn tapped me on the shoulder and pointed. A young nun in a gray habit was entering the courtroom. "May we approach, Your Honor?"

As the judge motioned us to come up, Hal whispered into Bennett's ear. When the lawyers were assembled in front of the bench the judge asked, "What is it, Mr. Elkins?"

"A new potential witness has just arrived," Flynn replied. "Mr. Elkins hasn't had the opportunity to speak to her. May we have a short recess?"

"That's nonsense, Judge. That so-called witness has nothing relevant she can testify to."

"Is that the nun who just entered the courtroom?"

"Yes," all three lawyers replied.

"Why didn't you prepare her before, Mr. Elkins?"

"He didn't know she'd be coming up from Texas," Flynn said.

"She can't add any admissible evidence, Judge," Bennett insisted.

"How do you know till you hear what she has to say?" Flynn replied.

At that moment the intercom on the bench buzzed, and the judge conferred for a minute, then turned back to us. "Gentlemen, something has come up that requires my immediate attention. We'll adjourn until tomorrow morning. Then we'll see if you decide to put her on. How long do you expect her to take?"

"Less than an hour, Judge," Flynn assured him.

"And is she your last witness?"

"Yes, Your Honor I said. If I put the sister on, we'll rest

right after she testifies."

"Mr. Bennett, be ready with your first witness for to-morrow morning."

"At what time, Judge? My first witness is my handwriting expert, and his time costs my client."

The judge looked at Bennett with mild disgust before turning to me. "Mr. Elkins, I assume you'll decided whether you'll be calling the nun by this afternoon."

Flynn and I both nodded.

"Please call Mr. Bennett this afternoon as soon as you decide."

"Yes, Your Honor."

WHEN THE CASE WAS ADJOURNED, Hal was the first person to get to Mary Elizabeth. "What the hell are you doing here?" he demanded.

Joe Bennett tried to pull him aside. "*Please*, Hal—the jury might hear you. Wait till they're all out of the room."

"Sister, I'm Algernon Flynn, and this is Ian Elkins. Can we go outside?"

"You'd better *watch* yourself, you *bitch*," Hal growled as he stomped off.

Over coffee, she discussed her possible testimony with us.

CHAPTER TWENTY-ONE

THAT EVENING, MARY CURRAN CAME HOME to find the light blinking on her answering machine. It was a message from Hal, and she immediately phoned Jason Kelly. "What did he say, Mrs. Curran?"

Her face reddened. "I can't use that language."

"Just give me the substance."

"He said that, if Mary Elizabeth testified tomorrow everything I owned would be invested in stock and junk bonds of companies that were going into bankruptcy."

". . .Does your brother have a power of attorney on your investments?"

"Yes, on two brokerage accounts."

"Call the brokers tomorrow morning first thing and tell

them you've canceled the power. Then call my secretary and give her the name and address of the brokers and your account numbers. We'll write them, and we'll also recommend another investment advisor."

"What about my daughter?"

"I'll call her now. I have the number of the convent she's staying at tonight."

THE NEXT MORNING, THE JURY was seated at 9:30. "As our last witness," I rose to say, "petitioner calls Sister Mary Elizabeth Curran."

"Will you swear or affirm to tell the truth, Sister?" Casey asked as he brought the bible to her.

"Either one, sir. I'm only going to tell the truth."

Bennett's face tightened.

The nun sat back in her chair with a serene expression. "Sister, were you related to James McGrath?"

"Yes, I'm his niece. My mother was his sister."

"Did you have any contact with your uncle James during his lifetime?"

"Oh, yes, quite a bit. Uncle Jim used to visit my mother several times a year, and I was usually able to get permission to come home to see the family's real estate mogul."

"Did you ever hear your uncle talk about your other uncles?"

"Objection," said Bennett. "Irrelevant and hearsay."

"It is *perfectly* relevant, Your Honor," I pointed out. "It goes to the decedent's state of mind. Besides, Mr. Bennett has waived that objection."

"How did he do that, Mr. Elkins?" the judge asked.

"He made no objection to Ms. Keller's testimony as to her uncles' opinion of his two brothers."

"I agree with you. Overruled.

"Oh, yes," the nun replied," Uncle Jim was a big talker."

"What did you hear him say about your uncle Harold McGrath?"

"He didn't like him. Thought he was a cheap, dumb, big- mouthed jock."

"Is that a quote?"

"Pretty much."

"What about your uncle Charlie McGrath?"

"In the beginning he didn't express much feeling about Charlie. Then he mentioned that he was working for him—helping to manage his buildings. About a year later, Mom asked about Uncle Charlie. She wanted to know how he was making out."

"What did your uncle Jim say?"

"He said Uncle Charlie was a stupid. . .I mean, a stupid person. I don't want to use the word."

"I understand, Sister. Did he say anything else?"

"Not that time, but a year later he told Mom he'd had to fire Charlie."

"Did he say why?"

"Yes. He said Uncle Charlie was taking bribes from his suppliers and letting them rip him off."

"Do you know how your uncle Jim felt about your cousin Alice?"

"He never said anything directly, but when he told us about firing Charlie, he told Mom that he'd given her Charlie's job as manager, so I assume that he must have liked her."

"*Objection!*" Bennett shouted. "Move to strike."

"Granted," said the judge. "Members of the jury, you must disregard the statement that Sister assumes that the decedent liked Ms. Keller. That is not evidence, and you may not consider it."

"Thank you, Sister. No further questions."

"Cross-examine, Mr. Bennett?"

The lawyer had a short, heated consultation with Hal, then turned to the witness. "Sister, isn't a fact that you are a member of the Convent of the Sacred Heart in Houston, Texas?"

"Yes, I am."

"And isn't it a fact that you claim that James McGrath promised to leave all or a large portion of his estate to your convent?"

"Yes, he did. He made that promise in my presence."

"And isn't it a fact that Alice Keller and your convent

made an arrangement that, if this claimed will is probated, there will be a substantial amount of money paid to the convent?"

"So I've been told."

"And wasn't that the price, the thirty pieces of silver, that is being paid for your lying testimony today?"

"*Objection!*" I practically shrieked. The first alternate juror crossed herself and appeared to be fingering her rosary beads.

Before the judge had time to rule, however, the young nun turned to him and said, "Your Honor, I want to answer that question."

"Then by all means do so."

"Mr. Bennett," she began, glaring at the lawyer, "I was brought up strictly in a good Christian home. I was taught that lying is a serious sin. I am a teacher in Catholic grade school, and I teach my children to tell only the truth. I will not lie under any circumstances."

The alternate juror smiled.

Bennett had another brief consultation with Hal, then turned to the jury with a sneer on his face. "No further questions."

I rested my case, and the judge motioned for us to come up to the bench.

"Okay, Mr. Bennett, the ball is now in your court. Will you be making a motion to dismiss now or will you just proceed with your case? I should point out that, from what I've seen, the petitioner has made out a *prima facie* case."

"I will be making a motion to dismiss, Judge."

"So be it," the judge replied, and we returned to our seats. "Ladies and gentlemen of the jury, the attorneys are about to make a motion in which you are not involved. Return to the jury room until you are recalled. Please don't discuss the case. When they had left, he said, "Mr. Bennett, make your motion."

For the next twenty minutes, Bennett spoke. His manner was low key, his presentation well-reasoned. Since there was irrefutable documentary proof that James McGrath was in the hospital on the day we claimed he had signed his will at Alice's apartment, he argued, no reasonable jury could find that the writing offered as his will could be anything other than a forgery.

My argument took less than five minutes: Alice had given a perfectly plausible explanation for McGrath's presence in her home, and the jury was entitled to make up its own mind.

"Gentlemen," the judge replied, "you both made very fine, well-reasoned arguments, and I enjoyed listening to them. I am going to deny the motion because, in my view, the petitioner has indeed made out a *prima facie* case. Certainly the hospital record is a very suspicious circumstance, but the explanation given by Ms. Keller was plausible and could be believed by a reasonable jury. This is not to say that, were I on the jury, I would believe the explanation, but that is a question that only the jury can answer. Another factor that could lead the jury to decide for Petitioner was the testimony of Sister Mary Elizabeth that the decedent didn't like his two brothers. As a businessman, it is unlikely he would want to die without a will, thereby allowing those two brothers to take half his estate. Motion denied."

"That's *bullshit!*" Hal shouted as he rose from his seat at the counsel table. "You don't know what the fuck you're talking about. You can't believe my lying bitch niece. She just wants to get Jim's money for her convent."

Bennett tried to pull him down to his seat and be quiet, but Hal resisted.

"*Mr. McGrath!*" the judge shouted, pounding his gavel. "You will sit down and be quiet, or I will have you jailed for contempt."

"But, Judge, can't you see she was lying through her teeth?" Hal continued as he began to calm down.

The judge glared at him, and Hal resumed his seat. "Mr. Bennett, are you ready to proceed?"

"Ready, Your Honor."

"Bring in the jury, Mr. Casey."

AFTER THE JURORS WERE SEATED, Bennett called his handwriting expert, Bruce Malone. As the tall, near-emaciated man made his way to the witness box, I noticed that he seemed to have changed since the deposition. He was wearing a jacket and tie, but that was to be expected. As he was being sworn, I finally realized what it was. The square-cut beard had been reshaped, trimmed down to a sharp point— a long goatee. It made him look even taller than he was. His testimony on direct was substantially identical to that in his deposition, except that Bennett brought out only the bare bones of his criminal conviction. He'd wanted to put in the full details so as to take away some of the sting from my cross but had made the mistake of telling Hal about his plans. The client had, at first, adamantly forbidden him from putting in anything, but finally consented to the fact of the conviction.

On cross I did indeed expose all the details of the crime and sentence, and stressed that Malone was extremely lucky he hadn't gone to prison. I nodded slowly. "Mr. Malone, isn't it a fact that, on your direct examination, you referred to only *five* exemplars of James McGrath's handwriting?"

"Yes, they were the best ones."

"But there were others, weren't there?"

"Yes, but not as good as the ones I identified."

"What was the total number of examples of Mr. McGrath's handwriting you saw?"

Malone's face tightened. "I don't recall the exact number."

"Approximately how many?"

"Maybe twenty."

"Show me the other fifteen."

"*Objection!*" Bennett shouted. "Irrelevant. We're relying on the exemplars that were put into evidence."

"Overruled. You should know better than that, Mr. Bennett. Show them to counsel, Mr. Malone."

The big man was shaken. "I. . .I don't have them with me."

". . .Where are they?" the judge demanded.

"In my file."

"Where's the file?"

"I'm not sure. It may be in my office."

"Where's your office?"

"In Yonkers."

"That's not very far from here. Go *get* it! It's nearly lunch time. We'll recess until 2:30."

"Your Honor," I said, "may we approach?"

"What is it, Mr. Elkins?" he whispered when we were in front o him.

"I would like to go with this witness to his office."

"Whatever for?" Bennett demanded.

"You know very well, Mr. Bennett. We want to have all of the exemplars of Mr. McGrath's handwriting before the jury. You should have offered them all on your direct case."

"I also suggest that we all travel together in one car to his office," I added.

"So ordered."

We all drove to Yonkers in Flynn's silver Lexus. On the way up, the atmosphere was frosty. Bennett and Malone sat in the back, engaging in whispered conversation; I sat up front. Flynn tried some small talk but got nowhere.

Malone's office was on the third floor of a small building in a run-down part of the business district. It consisted of a windowless ten-by-fifteen-foot room containing a battered wooden desk, shelves on standards behind it, and four six-drawer vertical files. The two visitor's seats were steel framed and covered in a nubby blue fabric, the high-backed desk chair in plush black leather. Malone first searched his cluttered desk and then the shelves. Finally he opened the middle drawer of the third filing cabinet. He went behind the *Mc* filing card and pulled out a red-rope envelope with *McGrath* on the label in red. He flipped through and withdrew an open folder marked *exemplars*. "This is it," he announced. The folder contained a small stack of hand-written papers.

I reached for it, but Bennett grabbed it first. "Not so fast, counselor. These are my client's property."

"That's okay, but I'm going to be next to you every minute till you hand it to the judge."

AT 2:30, WE WERE BACK IN COURT without the benefit of lunch. Five minutes later the court officer called the court to order, and the judge ascended the bench. "Here are the records you requested, Your Honor," Bennett said.

"Okay, let's call in the jury."

"Excuse me, Your Honor," I said, "but may I examine the documents before we get started?"

"You've had nearly three hours to read them, Mr. Elkins," the judge replied with a slight growl.

"Mr. Bennett did an exemplary job of withholding them from me."

"Grow up, Mr. Bennett," the judge muttered. "Read them over, Mr. Elkins, and tell me when you're ready," he continued, handing over the folder.

Flynn, Alice and I read the papers. Included were two insulting letters from James McGrath to his brother Hal, one of which referred to "your crooked brother, Charlie."

I then resumed my cross by having Malone identify each of the papers as specimens of James McGrath's handwriting, given to him by Hal McGrath, that the witness had used in connection with his examination of will. The papers were admitted into evidence. I showed one of the exhibits to Malone and asked, "Is this one of the exemplars of James McGrath's handwriting that you used to compare with the will and form your opinion as to its genuineness?"

"Yes."

"Please read it out loud to the jury."

"*Objection!*" Bennett shouted.

The judge motioned us up to the bench and then read the paper. "Is your objection that the letter is not relevant and is highly prejudicial, Mr. Bennett?"

"Yes, Your Honor."

"Sustained. That is not how you get the contents of this paper to the jury."

"Your Honor," Bennett interjected, "I move to strike the admission of Petitioner's exhibits 4J and K. They should not be shown to the jury."

The judge read the other letter. "Granted. Petitioners 4J and K are stricken from evidence. Unless you can establish a relevant connection for them, Mr. Elkins, they will not be shown to the jury. Ask your next question."

I had a hurried conference with Flynn before saying, "I have no further questions for this witness at this time, Your Honor, but I request that he be ordered to remain available for further examination if needed."

"On what basis?"

"I want to have my expert witness examine these documents. Then I may have additional questions."

"Granted. Call your next witness, Mr. Bennett."

"Your Honor, may I have a brief recess? I'm not sure whether we will be calling any other witnesses."

"I'd like one too, Your Honor," I added. "I want to

check on my expert."

"We'll recess for half an hour."

After the judge and jury had departed, Bennett and his two clients borrowed the deposition room for a conference. A half hour later they returned. As they came through the door, Hal turned to his lawyer. "You'd better be right."

"Don't worry, I am."

"But how am I going to counter that lying bitch if I don't testify?"

"You can't, but we've got to keep those papers out."

When the trial resumed, Bennett announced, "Objectants rest."

"Rebuttal, Mr. Elkins?"

"Yes, Your Honor. Petitioner calls Harold McGrath."

The big man waddled up to the stand.

After he was sworn, I said. "Your Honor, I request leave to treat Mr. McGrath as a hostile witness."

"Objection!" Bennett declared. "There's no evidence that Mr. McGrath is in any way hostile."

"Come on, Mr. Bennett, be serious. Overruled." The judge told the jury. "Ladies and gentlemen, so that you understand what has just happened, by allowing Mr. Elkins to treat Mr. McGrath as a hostile witness, I have merely permitted him to ask leading questions. They are not evidence, and you are to draw no inferences from that permission." The judge scratched his nose. "You may proceed, Mr.

Elkins."

"Mr. McGrath, isn't it a fact that you and your brother Charles were on very bad terms with James McGrath?"

"*Objection!*"

The judge motioned counsel to the bench.

"Judge, that's not a proper reply. We didn't bring anything about the decedent's feelings about my clients."

The judge turned to me. "What do you say to that, Mr. Elkins?"

"Will you let it in, subject to connection, Judge?"

"Overruled subject to connection. Answer the question, Mr. McGrath."

Hal looked puzzled.

"Do you want the question read back to you, Mr. McGrath?"

Hal shook his head then smiled. "No, I remember it. No, my brother Jim and I got along very well. He loved me and Charlie, and we loved him."

"Didn't you hear your niece Sister Mary Elizabeth say otherwise?"

"Yeah, but. . . ."

"Yeah but what?"

"The bitch is lying."

Bennett grimaced as he turned his head away from the jury.

I seized two pieces of paper from the reporter's desk.

"Mr. McGrath, I show you Petitioner's Exhibit 4J for identification." He handed one of the pieces of paper to Hal.

Is this a letter your brother James wrote you?"

"Yeah."

"And this is one of the examples of James's handwriting you gave Mr. Malone in connection with his examination of the will?"

"Yes."

"Please read it out loud to the jury."

"Objection."

"Overruled. Read it out loud, Mr. McGrath."

"'Dear Hal. How dare you talk about me to Mary that way. If you ever say any thing like that again, I'll sue you for slander. Jim.'"

"I offer it into evidence."

"Admitted."

"Now, Mr. McGrath, I show you Petitioner's Exhibit 4K for identification." I handed Hal the other piece of paper. "Is this another letter your brother James wrote you?"

"Yes," Hal whispered.

"I didn't hear you. Speak up."

"*Yes.*"

"And was *this* one of the samples of your brother's writing you gave to Mr. Malone to use in his examination of the will?"

"Yes."

"Please read it out loud to the jury."

Bennett's objection was again overruled.

"'Dear Hal. How dare you ask me to give Charlie back his job? Don't you know your crooked brother, Charlie, has been stealing from me? If he needs a job, then you give it to him. But you won't do that, will you? No, you're too fucking cheap. Jim.'"

I asked Hal no further questions, and Bennett decided not to try to rehabilitate his client on cross. Since my handwriting expert hadn't arrived, the judge adjourned the trial to the next day.

CHAPTER TWENTY-TWO

A S SHE EMERGED FROM THE TAXI that had brought her from the airport, Sister Mary Elizabeth considered how fortunate she was to be back where she belonged. It wasn't as though the sisters in New York hadn't been hospitable; they had treated her like a queen. Compared to her spartan cell in Houston, the accommodation in the convent in Manhattan was like a resort hotel. The sisters had kidded her about a projected alteration in which they would get an Olympic-sized pool, an exercise room, a sauna, and a nine-hole golf course. Even her part in the trial, although stressful, had been interesting; but she was glad to be home that late morning. At the front desk she was greeted by the chubby, motherly duty nun. "Good to see you, dear. Did you have a nice trip?"

"Yes, thank you, Sister Veronica, and God Bless, but it's good to be back."

"You have a telephone message from your aunt."

"Who?"

"She said she was your Aunt Carol. She left a number and asked that you call her."

Mary Elizabeth wondered what machinations Uncle Hal was engineering. He didn't have the guts to call himself, so he'd unleashed his poor, drunk wife on her. She returned the call and left a message on the answering machine. Carol called again during evening prayers, and the telephone tag ended at nine-thirty. "Hello, Aunt Carol. How are you?"

"Pretty well, thank God. And you, dear?"

"Just fine, thank you."

"It's been a long time since we've seen each other."

"Yes, it has," the nun replied. Her uncle's wife was having a difficult time getting to the point, but while Mary Elizabeth felt sorry for the woman, she decided to let her suffer her way through. For the next ten minutes Carol McGrath fumbled over a discussion of family matters, politics, the weather, and other things wholly unrelated to the purpose of her call. Her slurred speech suggested the number of drinks she'd needed in order to find the courage to pick up the phone. Finally, Mary Elizabeth took pity on her. "Look,

Aunt Carol, what did Uncle Hal ask you to call me about?"

The older woman breathed a sigh of relief. "Yes, dear, he did ask me to call. Not that I don't enjoy speaking to you."

"I know. What does he want?"

"He was very bothered by what you said in court."

"I know. He told me so—what does he want?"

"He wants you to take back what you said and—and . . . ."

"And what?"

"And tell the truth."

"I *did* tell the truth—the *absolute* truth."

"He says you didn't, but if you tell the truth now, he'll do something for you."

"What's the bribe he's offering for my immortal soul?" She heard weeping at the other end of the phone and felt badly. Being married to Hal was certainly a big enough cross to bear. "Don't cry, Aunt Carol."

"Thank you, dear," the older woman replied after blowing her nose. "He says he'll make a contribution to your convent."

"Look, Aunt Carol, I'm not for sale, and neither is the convent."

"He thought you'd say that, but you'd better do what he says."

"Why?"

"'Cause if you don't, he'll. . .hurt you."

"What's he going to do? Come to the convent and beat me up?"

"Oh, *no*, he'd never do that. But he *is* handling your mother's investments."

"Not any more, he isn't. Mother took him off all her accounts. Please tell Uncle Hal to stop using you to commit a crime."

After she'd hung up, Mary Elizabeth called Jason Kelly and told him.

THE NEXT MORNING, COURT CAME TO ORDER promptly at 9:30. Bennett and the McGraths were seated at the objectant's counsel table. My table was incomplete. Alice and I were present, as was our handwriting witness, but Algernon Flynn wasn't there. When Bennett answered ready, the judge looked at me. "Well, Mr. Elkins, are you ready to proceed?"

"Not quite, your honor. Mr. Flynn hasn't arrived. I assume he was caught in the Cross-Westchester traffic."

"I'm sure you can proceed without him."

At that moment the courtroom door opened and a slightly breathless Algernon Flynn swept in.

"Aha," said the judge. "Here he is. Let's proceed."

"Excuse me, Your Honor," said Flynn as he removed his Burberry. "May we have a short conference in your robing room?"

Judge Carter eyed him.

"I have something to bring before Your Honor that should be done in private."

"Very well. Counsel, come to my room."

When we were seated, he lit a small cigar. "What is it, Mr. Flynn?"

"First of all, Your Honor, I want to apologize for my tardiness."

Judge Carter shrugged.

"I called my office on my cell phone just as I reached the courthouse and was told I had an urgent message from counsel for the Houston archdiocese, so I immediately returned the call."

"And?" asked the judge with a touch of impatience.

"I spoke to Jason Kelly of that office, who told me that there has been some witness tampering."

"That's *nonsense*, Judge," Bennett declared.

The judge held up his hand. "Continue, Mr. Flynn."

"He told me that Mrs. Harold McGrath had called Sister Mary Elizabeth, offered a bribe for her to change her testimony, and threatened her mother with financial ruin if she didn't accede."

"Mr. Bennett," the judge barked, "I will not have such conduct in my court."

"I know nothing about this, Judge. May I have the opportunity to speak to my client?"

As Hal and Bennett entered the robing room, the judge said, "Mr. McGrath, I've heard some very disturbing things about you."

Hal glared but said nothing.

The judge turned towards Flynn. "Tell him what you've just told me."

He did.

"Well?" asked the judge, maintaining eye contact. "What do you have to say for yourself?"

"I don't understand what you mean, Judge. I didn't think there was anything wrong with telling my lying niece to tell the truth."

"Mr. McGrath, what you said, or had your wife say, was a lot more than that. You offered her a bribe, and you threatened her."

"Not at all. Mary Elizabeth knows I'm going to be making a contribution to her convent when I get my share of Jim's estate. My wife was just reminding her that, if the will goes through, there won't be any share to make that contribution from."

"What about the threat?"

"I didn't make any. I just pointed out that I was helping her mother with her investments, and that she was paying back my kindness by lying."

"Mr. McGrath, that's a lot of crap, and you know it. I think I have an obligation to report this to the district attorney."

"Do what ever you think is right, Judge," replied Hal with an infuriating smile.

"Okay, let's get on with the trial—and, Mr. Bennett, I suggest you control your client."

"But, Your Honor, I thought he gave a very plausible explanation. . . . Just like Ms. Keller gave for the decedent's presence at her apartment."

The judge gritted his teeth.

Petitioner's last witness was Mario Gambi. While he had followed the letter of the dress instructions given him by wearing a suit, he hadn't quite gone along with the spirit. I nearly choked when the witness walked into the courtroom in a fluorescent green outfit edged with leather piping, a red silk shirt with a flowered tie, and alligator boots. I led him through his criminal conviction, including the prison term. The balance of his testimony was substantially identical to that given on his deposition.

On cross, Bennett leaned heavily on the criminal record, pounding it home with frequent repetition, and by the end the jurors appeared quite sorry for the poor witness. Bennett hadn't wanted to do it, but Hal had insisted.

After Gambi left the box, I announced, "Petitioner rests."

The judge motioned the lawyers up to the bench. "Mr. Bennett, I assume you're going to make a motion to dismiss."

"Yes, Your Honor."

"Okay. I have a number of matters I must take care of this afternoon, so I'm going to dismiss the jury, and we'll have closing arguments tomorrow morning after which I'll charge the jury. I will expect your requests to charge by nine-thirty tomorrow morning."

Once the jury had been sent home, Bennett argued his motion to dismiss, how McGrath couldn't have signed the will at Alice's apartment when he was in the hospital, how her story was unbelievable, how my jailbird expert couldn't be believed. This time he wound down in less than ten minutes.

As I was about to respond, the judge held up his hand. "I don't need to hear your arguments, Mr. Elkins. You've made out a *prima facie* case, and it's up to the jury to decide who they're going to believe. Motion denied."

RETURNING FROM COURT, I STARTED to prepare for my closing argument. I knew it would probably make or break the case. I outlined some thoughts on a yellow legal pad but, after a few minutes, found I couldn't concentrate. I needed a change of scenery, a little diversion. "Just where do you think you're going, Mr. Elkins?" chirped the office manager, Rosemary Lennon as I marched to the door with my massive trial bag. "This is a law office—not a bank, or are you going to night court?"

"I didn't know your were a descendant of Simon Legree, Rosie."

She chuckled, setting off a ripple on her triple chin. "Seriously, where are you going? The boss likes to know."

"You can tell Mr. Rooney that I'm having trouble putting my closing statement together, so I'm going to Riverdale to consult with an expert on making noise."

"I assume that would be the young Miss Elkins."

"You're quite correct, Rosie. When you're short on words, ask a woman."

"Good idea, Mr. Elkins, and give my regards to Mrs. Elkins and the little darling."

A half hour later, I had parked my Volvo three blocks from the co-op and was entering my apartment.

"My, you're home early, Mr. Elkins," remarked the baby nurse I'd hired for Helen's first week home.

"Thought I'd get a change of scenery. How's the little princess?"

"Just wonderful," she replied in her Jamaican lilt. "Mrs. Elkins is nearly finished nursing, and I'll be going in to change her in a few minutes. Want to watch the show?"

"I wouldn't miss it for the world—I'd better learn how to do it before you leave."

"We have a visitor," announced the tall, slim nurse with a medium complexion after knocking on the bedroom door.

"Who is it, my mother?"

"I don't think so. He doesn't look like her. He looks more like the young lady's father. Are you decent?"

"Send him in. He's seen me like this before." When we entered, Helen was sitting up in bed, the baby in her lap busily sucking on her right breast. "What brings you home so early?"

"Do I need an excuse to see my two favorite ladies?"

"Sometimes I wonder. How's the trial going?"

I shrugged and raised my palms. "We're nearly done. I'll be summing up tomorrow morning, but I can't make an outline of what I'm going to say."

"Tell them some jokes."

"What're you, on the other side? Want me to lose the case?"

"I thought jokes were your specialty—a regular stand-up comic."

"If I had to make a living on my jokes, we'd starve."

She lifted the baby off her breast and over her left shoulder.

"I didn't know you had to burp babies who're being breast fed."

"Oh, yes, Mr. Elkins," said the nurse. "It's less likely for nursing babies to suck up air, but it can happen easy enough."

As if on cue, the infant belched loudly and spit up a

small amount onto the diaper on Helen's shoulder.

"You see?" Helen declared. "Right from the horse's mouth. I think she's taken all she can get now, so I guess we'd better change her."

"Why don't we let Mr. Elkins do it?" asked the nurse.

"Good idea," replied Helen. "It'll broaden his horizons."

WE HAD BARBECUED SEA BASS FOR DINNER, with plantain and okra. I'm going to miss her when she leaves," said Helen. "She's added a new dimension to my cooking."

As we ate, Helen brought up the trial again. "Any luck in outlining your closing statement?"

"I keep trying, but the words won't come."

"You know what you want to say. You've been living with case almost forever. Why don't you just get up in front of the jury and wing it? The words will come."

"You're probably right, but I can't operate that way. I'm much more comfortable with a sheet with some notes on it, even if I never look at them."

She thought for a minute. Her face brightened. "Tell you what. When we're done, sum up to me. Make believe I'm the jury. I'll make some notes as you talk. You can use them, or at least they'll be a starting point."

I embraced her. "I'm lucky you married me."

"Hey, Mister Lawyer, are you going to do that to the

jury?"

"I will if they go my way."

WHEN ALGERNON FLYNN RETURNED to his office, the receptionist told him that Mr. Donovan wanted to see him. In the managing partner's office, Matt Bowen was seated in one of the visitor's chairs. Both partners were sipping scotch from ice-filled lo-ball tumblers. Donovan appeared to be in a jovial mood. "Hello, my boy. How are you?"

"Just fine, sir."

"Help yourself to a nip," the older man continued, pointing to a tray with an ice bucket, several glasses, and a bottle of Glenlivet. Flynn did and took a seat next to Bowen.

"How's the trial going?" asked Donovan after the young man had taken a few sips.

"Everyone's rested, and we'll be making closing statements tomorrow."

"And?"

"And what, sir?"

"And how're we *doing*? Are we going to win?"

"Too close to call."

"What about the contingency plan?" Donovan asked, eyeballing the associate.

"I have what you bought."

"How are you going to use it?"

"I've had a private discussion with Ms. Keller."

Donovan looked at him quizzically.

"She's the niece who's probating the current will," Matt Bowen told him.

"And?"

"And if the jury comes in against her, she will say that she's just found another will."

"Where did she find it?" Bowen asked.

"Misfiled in one of the real estate company's files."

"How're you going to probate the new will? Who will testify?" Bowen inquired.

Flynn smiled. "We were very lucky. Two of my law school classmates went into partnership a few years ago. They sublet some space on the ninety-seventh floor of Two World Trade Center. I was the secretary of my law school fraternity, and I just happen to have several samples of their handwriting and signatures."

Donovan smiled broadly. "They died on September 11, and the entire contents of their office was destroyed."

The young man nodded. Matt Bowen remained in his partner's office after Flynn had left. "I don't like this, Jerry."

"Sounds like a sensible plan."

"If it backfires, we're going to be in a lot of trouble."

Donovan shook his head. "Not *we*. *Him*."

"If the cardinal knew what we were doing, he wouldn't approve."

Donovan smiled. "I'm sure he wouldn't say so, but underneath it all, he'd know that the needs of the Church come ahead of mere technicalities."

Donovan shook his head after Bowen had returned to his office. "My so-called partner is much too squeamish," he mumbled.

CHAPTER TWENTY-THREE

W
HEN THE COURT CAME TO ORDER at 9:30, the judge immediately called Bennett and me into his robing room, together with his law secretary, Frank McCullough. He was all business—no cigar or coffee. "I'll take your requests to charge, gentlemen." We each handed up thin packets of paper, which he handed to McCullough and gave him an hour for comments.

The law secretary nodded, scratched his blonde beard, and left.

"Okay, gentlemen—after your summations, Frank and I will fill you in on what I'm going to charge so you can protect your record."

We expressed our thanks for his consideration.

Back in the courtroom, the jury was summoned. When they had taken their seats, he said. "Ladies and gentlemen, you are about to hear the closing statements of the lawyers, in which they will try to convince you to decide the case for their respective clients. What they say is not evidence. Only the sworn testimony you heard from the witness box—" he pointed— "and the documents admitted into evidence may be considered by you. Since the petitioner, who is attempting to prove the will, has the burden of proof, her lawyer's closing arguments will come last. Mr. Bennett," he concluded.

Joe Bennett's argument stressed the unlikelihood of Alice's story. He concluded: "As you have been told, James McGrath was a wealthy man, and an intelligent and successful businessman. Is it likely that Mr. McGrath would dispose of his large estate by a will that was not drawn by a lawyer? Is it likely that he would have the will prepared by his niece, who is the chief beneficiary, and witnessed by her boyfriend? Does it make sense to you that he took a personal leave of absence from the hospital where he was recovering from a heart attack to go to a party at his niece's apartment, and then take a taxi back? I suggest to you that, if he wanted to see his nieces, he had only to call them on the telephone and ask them to visit him in the hospital. I suggest to you, ladies and gentlemen, that you have been fed a packet of obvious lies, and I'm sure you're too intelligent to swallow them. Don't allow that designing woman to pull the wool over your eyes. There is only one sensible verdict—to deny probate to this false will."

WHEN HE FINISHED, I APPROACHED the lectern. In keeping with my nature, my argument was low keyed. I stressed that smart businessmen do odd things, and that it would be highly unusual that James McGrath would die without a will and allow half his large estate to go to brothers he strongly disliked. In finishing my argument I used the opening Bennett gave me.

"Ladies and gentlemen, Mr. Bennett's just asked you some questions that I would like to help you answer." I looked down at my notes. 'Is it likely that Mr. McGrath would dispose of his large estate by a will that was not drawn by a lawyer?' Yes, perfectly likely. He was a landlord of apartment houses in poor neighborhoods. While he undoubtedly used lawyers to dispossess tenants who were behind in their rent, he doesn't seem to have been the sophisticated type of person who'd use a lawyer for everything. Maybe he *should* have had a lawyer draw his will, but it makes perfect sense for him to have done it himself. Mr. Bennett's second question was: 'Is it likely that he would have the will prepared by his niece, who is the chief beneficiary, and witnessed by her boy friend?' Again the answer is, *perfectly* likely. Alice Keller worked for him. Why *wouldn't* he use her to prepare the will? Was he supposed to type it himself? As to the witnesses, who better than the boyfriends of his nieces? They were at the birthday party. Mr. Bennett's last question was: 'Does it make sense to you that he took a personal leave of absence from the hospital where he was recovering from a heart attack to go to a party at his niece's apartment and then take a taxi back?' Again the answer is, it makes perfect sense. Mr. McGrath was an entrepreneur. He ran his own business and was used to having things his way. If he felt well enough to go to a birthday party, he'd go. Maybe you or I would be afraid to just walk out of a hospital, but James McGrath wouldn't, and he did. Can you picture the poor man now, wondering whether you're going to give half of his very substantial estate to two brothers he had no use for? No, ladies and gentlemen, while Mr. Bennett is correct that 'there is only one sensible verdict,' his conclusion is wrong. The only sensible verdict is to grant probate to the will so that James Mc-Grath's property can go where *he* wanted it to go."

WE WERE CALLED BACK INTO THE ROBING ROOM. The judge was alone, seated behind his desk, smoking another of his small cigars. "Well, gentlemen, you've each made a credible argument. Frank McCullough's dropped off his memo on the charge, and I've got to go over it. When it's firmed up, Frank will brief you on it in his office. In the meantime, I'd like to make a suggestion to you. In my opinion, you're running close to a dead heat. While I'm very curious to see how this ends, I wouldn't want to be the lawyer whose client comes in second. I'm going to send the jury out for an early lunch. I would suggest that each of you speak to your clients and try to convince them that a settlement makes more sense than a verdict against them. I'll have the jury return at two. I want you to report to me at one about whether or not we can resolve this case. If we can't, then Frank can brief you, and I'll charge the jury."

"WHY THE HELL *SHOULD* I?" Alice asked as she caught the waiter's eye and pointed to her coffee cup.

"Because more is better than less, " I said flatly.

The waiter brought a carafe and filled all three cups. "How's the Danish?" Algernon Flynn inquired.

"You'd be better off with the Greek pastry."

"Me, too," Alice added.

"And you, sir?"

I shook my head. "No, thanks. I've got to keep my girl-ish figure.

"What'd you *mean* by that?" she asked after the waiter left.

"By what?" I sipped my coffee.

"About more being better than less."

"That you'll get more in a settlement than if the jury comes in against us."

"But I'll get more if the jury comes in for me."

"If, and it's a big if." Flynn cut off a piece of his pastry, stabbed it with his fork, and brought it delicately to his mouth.

She pushed her plate away. "Why?"

"Because he was in the *hospital*," I replied.

"I explained all of that."

I shook my head. "Come off it, Alice. It was a good try, but if you were on the jury, would *you* buy it?"

She offered no response.

"If you'd only told me in the beginning, we could have done something about it."

"What?"

"Checked the hospital records, maybe gotten in touch with the doctor, one of the nurses."

"It was too long ago. You'd never find them, or they wouldn't remember."

"Even so, it wouldn't have looked as bad if you'd been up front with it."

She sighed. "So you think we've got a loser?"

"We're definitely on the short side."

"What do you suggest?"

"Offer them a third and settle for a half, or even two-thirds."

"What do you think, Al?"

Flynn nodded.

She sat deep in thought for a few minutes. Then her face brightened. "I think the two of you are ganging up on me. I'd like to discuss it with each of you separately—one on one. Then I'll make up my mind."

I shrugged. "Okay with me."

"Why don't you two start?" Flynn asked. "I've got to use the facilities."

While he was away, Alice and I went over the same scenario. When he returned I followed suit. Once I was out of earshot, she turned to Flynn. "What about our alternate plan?"

"What about it? If we lose, we'll try it."

"Then why should I settle?"

"Please, Alice. The new will plan is *far* from perfect. The object isn't to *try* the new case."

"Then what *is* the object?"

"To force your stupid uncles to agree to a reasonable settlement."

"Why should they do it?"

He shook his head. "Because, having won the first case, they'd be faced with the prospect of having to try another one."

"So you think I should settle?"

"If you can."

"Okay,"she said when I returned to the table. "You guys convinced me. I'll give it a try."

"And offer a third?" I asked

"That's right," she replied brightly. Then her face clouded over. "What about my Aunt Mary?"

"She'll go for it," Flynn replied. "It'll benefit the convent."

AT 1:00, FLYNN, BENNETT, AND I MET with the judge in the robing room. "Well, how did you make out? Can this be settled?"

"I think there's room for discussion, Judge." I told him.

"What about your clients, Mr. Bennett?"

"I have a little bit of movement." Bennett had a pained expression on his pudgy face.

"What do you mean by that?"

"If Ms. Keller will drop the probate, my clients will consent to all legals, fixed by your honor, to come off the top."

"And your client, Mr. Elkins?"

"She doesn't object to legals coming off the top, but she wants to limit her aunt and uncles to one-third of their intestate share."

"What do you say, Mr. Bennett?"

"I don't think my clients will go for it, but I'll speak to them."

"No. bring them in." As Bennett left, the judge turned to Flynn and me. "Is there any room beyond the third?"

"I don't know, Judge," I replied. "I think my client

would like to hear a response from her uncles before she considers any further movement."

"Okay, you two wait outside until I speak to Bennett's clients."

"So, gentlemen," he said when Bennett and the Mc-Graths were seated before him. "I understand your niece made has you an interesting offer."

"Yeah," replied Hal. "She's offering to steal my brother's estate from me."

"She's offering you something. How much will it take to make a deal? Remember, if the jury comes in for her, you get nothing and have to pay your own legals."

"She can go straight to hell."

Charlie nudged his brother's shoulder.

"Yeah?"

"What if we lose and get nothing?"

"Shut up, you little bastard."

The judge smiled at Hal. "Mr. McGrath, your brother has just as much right to his say as you have."

"The hell he does. I've fronted all the money. If he wants to settle, he can pay it all out of his share. Why should I give any part of my share to her?"

"Because the jury can come in against you."

"But Jim was in the *hospital*. He *couldn't* have signed the will in her apartment."

"She explained that."

"You don't believe that bullshit, do you, Judge?"

"It doesn't matter what I believe. The question is what the jury believes."

"They can't be that stupid."

The judge shrugged and raised his palms. "Okay, Mr. McGrath, if that's what you want, the jury will have to decide."

LATER THAT AFTERNOON, THE JUDGE charged the jury on the law and sent them out to deliberate. With nothing to do but wait, we all sat around the courtroom and twiddled our thumbs. I had brought materials to read, but I was too keyed up to concentrate. After the first hour, a message came back from the jury. They wanted to see the hospital record and have Alice's explanation read to them, then went back to their room.

During one of his trips to the men's room, I found myself alone with Joe Bennett, who sighed, "I *hate* this waiting."

"Me, too. But it comes with the job."

"You know, there's something I've meaning to say to you."

"Oh?"

"I've been climbing on your back all through this case."

I nodded. "You *have* sort of made it personal."

"I know, and I shouldn't have. Justin said some things

about you, and I guess I wanted to believe them. But you've been decent and straightforward all the way through, and while I don't wish you any success in this case, I really have nothing against you."

"Or me against you. We both have very difficult clients, and we're only doing a job."

"You can say that again. Our clients are real bastards, but we don't have to be," Bennett replied, and offered his hand.

At four forty-five the judge called the jury into the courtroom. "Well, ladies and gentlemen, are you close to a verdict?"

"No, Judge," replied the foreman, a middle aged bank teller. "We're pretty well deadlocked."

"Do you think another half or three-quarters of an hour will allow you to resolve it?"

"No, sir. Not a chance."

"Very well, we'll adjourn the case until tomorrow at nine-thirty. I'm going to send you home, but please don't discuss this case with anyone. Not even your family."

AT 7:30 THAT EVENING, THE PHONE RANG in Harold Mc-Grath's hotel room. "Yeah," he answered, putting down his second can of Bud since dinner. He was staying at a third-rate hotel in downtown White Plains where there wasn't a damn thing to do at night except stare at four walls and drink. At least it was better than the room at the Y he'd gotten for Charlie.

"It's me, Carol," said the slurred voice on the other side.

"I know. What're you, drunk again?"

"I've only had a few."

"A few dozen, I'll bet. What're you calling about?"

"Can't a woman call her own husband?"

"Cut the crap. You don't like me any more than I like you."

"How's the case going?"

He picked up the can from the night table and stared at the wet ring it had left. "It's with the jury now."

"Are you going to win?"

"I thought so, but they've been out all afternoon and can't make up their minds. The judge says it's a fifty-fifty case, but I think he's nuts."

"Won't they settle?"

"The bitch offered me a third of what I'd get without the will, and I'm sure she'll give more."

"And?"

"And I told her to take a walk. What's this all about?"

"I think you might want to reconsider."

"Why?

"You just got a call from Jerry Hendricks, who manages the property you two have downtown."

"So?

"He said there were some violations put on the building, and it's going to cost a lot to get them taken care of."

"Oh, shit. Give me Jerry's number."

CHAPTER TWENTY-FOUR

W HERE'S MR. BENNETT?" THE JUDGE ASKED at 9:30 the next morning after striding industriously to his chair and finding the attorney's seat unoccupied.

"I don't know, Judge," said Hal. "I tried to call him last night, but I couldn't get in touch with him."

"We'll wait a little while. He must have been caught in traffic."

"He probably was, Your Honor," I replied. "The Cross-Westchester was a mess this morning. If I hadn't left real early, I'd probably have been late, too."

The judge nodded. "Okay. I'll be in my robing room. Call me when he gets here. In the meantime, the jury can start deliberating."

"Okay, Judge. I think they're doing it now," the court officer said,

After the judge left, Hal waddled over to Alice. "How're you doing, my girl?"

"I haven't been your girl in a long time. What do you want?"

"I thought, us being family and all, that maybe we ought to stop this. Why don't we step outside and get away from these bums?"

She turned to Al and me. "Should I be talking to him without you?"

"You can," I said. "Listen to him, but don't say anything before you discuss it with us."

They sat together on a bench in the hallway just opposite the courtroom door. "So how've you been, Alice?"

She sniffed and nearly gagged. His breath was loathsome. "I'm okay. What did you want to offer?"

"Come on, Alice, don't be like that. We're family, and I want to keep it that way."

"Fine. We're in the middle of a lawsuit, and you want to settle it. What's your offer?"

Hal saw red and was tempted to slap her silly. With great effort, he held himself in check. "Look, dear, what do you want?"

Alice shook her head. "You already have my offer.

Now it's up to you."

"What offer?"

"The one you turned down flat," said Bennett as he got off the elevator. "What's going on around here?"

"My niece and I were having a friendly family chat."

The lawyer took Hal by the arm and tugged him toward the courtroom door. "Let's talk inside, after I check in."

"Where the hell've you been?" Hal asked, following him into the courtroom.

"Traffic on the Cross-Westchester."

"What about last night? I tried calling you for hours."

"I had a dinner meeting." Bennett checked in with the court officer, then led Hal to the back of the courtroom. "Now, what's going on?"

Hal filled him in.

"I think you're right. We *should* try to settle it. Actually we should have a long time ago."

"You think we're going to lose?" Hal had a concerned look on his face.

"No, we've got the better case—but it's far from a shoe-in."

"What do you think our chances are?"

"Maybe sixty-forty. They would have been better if you'd let me try it the way I wanted to and not made the jury angry with us."

Hal put on a contrite expression.

"So what do you want to do?"

"I guess I should make her an offer."

"How much? So far, all you've offered is to have the legals come off the top if she'd drop the case."

"How about five?"

"Five what?"

"Five thou."

"From each of you?""

"No, total."

"Don't do it. That's like spitting in her face. It'll only make her furious."

Hal's chins wiggled as he shook his head. "Let me talk to Charlie."

THAT DAY AT THE SACRED HEART SCHOOL, Sister Mary Elizabeth entered the principal's office. "You called me, Sister?" she asked her near cadaverous sixty-year-old, superior.

"Yes, Sister. Please have a seat."

Mary Elizabeth did so, on a blue steel-framed visitor's chair in front of the battered wooden desk.

"You will recall, Sister, that it has become nearly impossible to find members of our order to fill teaching vacancies in this institution?"

Mary Elizabeth found it difficult to keep a straight face but strained to do so. Sister Mary Robert had become a legend in her own time. Her long-winded, overly formal pronouncements, even when addressed to close friends, had earned her the title of *Sister Pontifica*. "Yes, Sister."

"And you are aware that Sister Bernadad will be retiring at the end of the spring semester, leaving us with an opening in the fourth grade?"

"Yes, Sister."

"We have decided to fill that vacancy in the fourth grade by promoting you into that position."

Mary Elizabeth groaned inwardly. She loved teaching the first grade and would have preferred staying there for the balance of her teaching career. "Thank you, Sister," she replied with minimal enthusiasm.

"This will be a step on your road to becoming the principal when I retire."

Mary Elizabeth's heart sank even deeper. She didn't want to be an administrator. Her vocation was teaching. Only the rule of obedience kept her from objecting. "Yes, Sister."

"We are considering hiring Helen Dolan, whom you interviewed last month, to teach your first-grade class."

"She'd be a good choice. She's student-taught two of my classes and did beautifully. The children reacted very well to her."

"I know that you think well of her. I was impressed with her resume and her Notre Dame transcript."

"Then you'll hire her?"

"It is very possible, but first I want to interview her and observe one of her classes."

"That's a good idea. When will you do it?"

"Today. She's scheduled to meet me in about an hour. After that she will teach your afternoon class."

"Wonderful," Mary Elizabeth said with forced enthusiasm. "After the interview, please ask her to come to the classroom. I'll give her my lesson plan and then take her out to lunch."

"No, that's not a good idea. I'm sure she likes you, and your help and presence will give her confidence. I want to see how she reacts under pressure."

Mary Elizabeth fought to suppress a grimace.

"What I want you to do is to return to the convent after the morning class. After the interview, I'll take Miss Dolan to the classroom, introduce her to the class, and stay with her until the end of the school day. When I bring her over, I want you to just leave."

"I assume that I'll first greet her."

"Absolutely *not*."

"This is Miss Dolan," the principal announced to the class at noon. "She will be your teacher for the rest of the day. Sister Mary Elizabeth, I believe you have some duties at the convent. You may leave now."

As Mary Elizabeth trudged back, she already knew that what Sister Mary Robert was doing would make it nearly impossible for poor Helen Dolan to perform at her best, and that they would lose an excellent teaching prospect. Perhaps it would be a good idea if she did become the next principal. When she reached the convent, she ran into Sister Veronica. "My, you're early, dear. Have you eaten your lunch?"

"No, Sister, I brought it back with me. I'll eat it in my cell."

"No need for that. The congregation are still at lunch. I'm sure there'll be enough for you."

"Thank you and God bless, Sister."

The stocky nun scratched her head. Suddenly, her face lit up. "By the way, you received a long-distance telephone call this morning."

"From whom?"

"A man with an accent. He sounded Jewish."

"What was his name?"

Sister Veronica looked in a pigeon hole to the right of her desk and pulled out a slip of paper. "Finkelstein. Isadore Finkelstein. He called from Florida and said he was a lawyer."

"Did he say what it was about?"

"Something about the convent."

"That's a bullshit offer, Joe. Is she out of her mind?"

"She's coming closer, Hal. Maybe if you got off your

high horse, she'd get more realistic."

"Yeah, Hal," Charlie added. "Let's try to settle this before the jury comes in. I really need *something* from this estate."

"Shut up, you little shit. I'm running this show."

"But, Hal—"

In light of a near murderous glare from his older brother, Charles McGrath lapsed into silence. The negotiations had been going on for most of the day while the jury deliberated. Rather than speak face to face, the lawyers had been shuttling back and forth with offers and counter-offers. Hal had started with dollar amounts, which Alice ignored. Near the end of the morning, he'd finally switched to percentages, starting with ninety-seven to three, and when he finally got to eighty-five to fifteen, Alice moved from thirty to thirty-five. The judge's law secretary had suggested fifty-fifty, but both of us turned him down flat.

BY 3:45 THEY WERE LOCKED at seventy-five from Hal and forty from Alice, and all of the lawyers were frustrated. "What was wrong with fifty-fifty?" I asked her.

"Nothing. I'd grab it in a minute, but Hal would never go for it, and if I agreed, it would only be sign of weakness."

"If I could get you sixty-forty his way, would you take it?"

"I don't know. How do you think you could get it?"

"Let me talk to Joe Bennett off the record. I have the feeling that's the figure he thinks it should settle at."

"Let me think about it for a while."

IN THE MEANTIME, BENNETT was engaged in discussion with his clients. "Hal, we've got to get off the stick before the jury comes in with something you might not like."

"So what should we do, give it away?"

"Of course not. What about the fifty-fifty?"

"Too low. You told me it was sixty-forty."

"If I can get you sixty-forty, will you take it?"

"I don't know. Let me think on it."

AT FOUR-THIRTY THE JUDGE called for the jury. When they had returned he asked the foreman, "Where do you stand? Are you close to a verdict?"

"I don't know, Judge. We're pretty well deadlocked."

"Do you think another day of deliberation would help?"

"It might. We've been having a lot of discussions, and there's been a little movement."

"Okay, I'll tell you what. I'm going to send you home now. Come back tomorrow morning, and sit 'til the lunch hour. If you haven't decided by then, or at least tell me that you're almost there, I'll declare a mistrial. But let me make myself clear— please try your hardest to decide. It would be a shame if you spent all this time for nothing."

AFTER DINNER THAT EVENING, SAM AND MOLLY visited their new granddaughter. Molly brought a care package of two cooked meals, pot roast and chicken *cordon bleu*. "So you shouldn't have to cook when the nurse leaves."

"Thanks, Mom. It wasn't necessary. Both Ian and I are perfectly capable cooks."

"Yeah," I added. "She's your daughter. How could she be anything but a first-class cook?"

"Stop arguing," Molly insisted. "I enjoy doing it."

The two grandparents took turns holding Carol until Regina came into the living room and announced it was the young lady's bedtime.

Since the baby and her nurse slept in the living room, we moved to the kitchen. I put up coffee and asked if anyone wanted anything stronger.

"A little brandy in the coffee would be nice," Sam replied.

"You shouldn't," Molly said. "You're driving, and remember what the doctor said."

"He only told me not to have too much. One won't hurt."

She shook her head.

"How's the big case going?" Sam asked me.

"Not so hot. The jury's been out nearly two days, and I'd guess we're on the short end."

"Why don't you settle it?"

"I'd like to, but both sides are stubborn. The judge told the jury that, if they weren't close to a verdict by lunchtime, tomorrow he was going to declare a mistrial and have the case retried."

"Stupid people. All cases should be settled. God only knows what a jury will say, and *He* won't tell."

THE NEXT MORNING THE PARTIES CONTINUED NEGOTIATING while the jury deliberated. At 11:00, Alice could take no more. "Look, Ian, if you can get a sixty-forty, I'll take it."

I wandered to the back of the courtroom and read some papers for ten minutes. At that point Bennett came out, heading toward the men's room, and I followed him. As we were washing our, hands, I said. "I have a suspicion that you and I are pretty close about what this case should settle for."

"It wouldn't surprise me."

"I don't have any authority to settle it, and I'm sure you don't, but we ought to exchange figures."

Bennett nodded, took a pen from his pocket, ripped off a sheet of towel, and scribbled some numbers. I did the same and we laid the sheets face up on a sink. "Okay," said Bennett. "Let's go back and try to jam it down their throats before the jury comes in."

We took our clients into separate parts of the hallway, and by 12:30 all had agreed that, subject to Mary's approval, the will would be probated, legals would come off the top, and Alice would get forty percent of her aunt and uncles' net share.

Casey stuck his head out of the door and announced, "The jury's coming in. Get inside."

As the jury was trooped in, Bennett spoke up. "Your Honor, may we have just a few moments?"

The judge motioned us up. "What is it, Mr. Bennett? Do you have a settlement?"

"Yes, subject only to Mary Curran's approval."

"Too late, counselor—the jury's in, and they've worked too hard to take it away from them now. Mr. Foreman," he demanded. "Do you have a verdict?

"Yes, Your Honor."

CHAPTER TWENTY-FIVE

A T THREE THAT AFTERNOON, MARK ROONEY'S intercom buzzed. He shifted his weight to the right side of his desk and picked up the phone. "Yes, Rosie."

"Mr. Elkins just got back from court."

"Ask him to come into my office."

Two minutes later I was seated in front of the great man with a cup of coffee in my hand. "What's the matter?" I asked, pointing to the black coffee Rooney was drinking unaccompanied by pastry.

"I had a checkup a few days ago. Doctor told me my pressure was way too high, and that, if I didn't lose some weight I'd get a heart attack or a stroke."

"I'm glad you're taking his advice. I wouldn't want anything to happen to you."

"Thanks, Ian. Kathy's been leaning on me too," Rooney took another sip of his coffee and made a face. "From your sad expression, I gather it didn't go too well."

"Nope. They denied probate five to one."

"Hey, you did better than I thought you would. If there'd been a bet going, I'd have taken six to nothing the first day. Were you able to find out why?"

"Yeah, I caught one of the jurors in the hall. She was my one. She said the hospital record killed me. Four of them didn't buy Alice's explanation from the beginning. She and the foreman held out for probate—they couldn't see McGrath wanting either Hal or Charlie to get anything. But the other four talked the foreman into going with them. She thinks he changed his vote to avoid a hung jury and sitting all that time for nothing."

"Damn shame. If she'd told you in the beginning, it might have worked out. . . . What about our fee? I guess we'd better make an application to have it paid out of the estate."

I shook my head. "It gets worse."

Rooney made a face. "How's *that* possible?"

"After the verdict, the judge called us into the robing room. He wanted to know whether we were going to make any motions against the verdict. Flynn said he didn't think so, because Alice had found another will misfiled in the company's papers. It leaves one-third to Alice and two-thirds to the convent. The judge jumped on me for not informing him sooner, but Flynn told him I didn't know about it. Alice had just told him. She didn't tell me because she was displeased with my services and was discharging me. I spoke up about what she owed us and wanted to have the court order it paid out of the estate. Flynn said that he would be making an application to have Alice reimbursed for her legals out of the estate, but that she objected to us getting anything additional and threatened to sue us for malpractice if we pressed our fee claim."

"Son of a bitch. That's weird."

"It gets weirder. The will was drawn by two law school classmates of Flynn, who died on September 11 in the World Trade Center."

"How're they going to prove the will?"

"He wouldn't say."

". . .Doesn't smell right to me."

"Me neither. When I asked Flynn for a copy, he clammed up, but it'll be available in a week. That's how much time the judge gave them to file the new will."

"Let's order a copy. In fact, you ought to pick one up."

"What are we going to do about our fee?"

"Let me sleep on it. A malpractice claim could send our rates sky high."

For the next several days I fell into a deep funk. Nothing amused me. My only solace was Helen and the baby. Things gradually brightened up, though, and I began to feel better.

ONE EVENING TWO WEEKS LATER, I was still in the office. I'd wanted to be home but, as usual, my jealous mistress, the law, took precedence. Only one more task, and I could leave. I looked up from the motion I was correcting and saw a flashing phone light on my cluttered desk. The last person in the office, I picked up. "Rooney and Associates."

"Is that you, Ian?"

"Yeah. Who's this."

"Al. Al Flynn."

Why is this son of a bitch calling me? I wondered. "How're you doing, Al?"

"Hanging in."

"How's the new McGrath will? Got it probated yet?"

I heard a faint laugh. "You're some kidder. But seriously, that's why I called."

"What can I tell you about that? I'd never heard of it till Alice fired me."

"Well, right now she and I can use your help."

I bristled. "Why should I help *her*? She fires me, won't pay what she owes, and threatens a malpractice?"

"She'll make it worth your while, so let's you and me talk. Can you meet me tonight for a drink?"

"Not tonight, Al."

"When?"

"I'll call you tomorrow."

"Let me give you my number."

"I have your office number."

"No not the office, my cell." He gave it to me and rang off.

I resumed my labors with mixed feelings. Should I even meet with Flynn? I'll talk to Mark tomorrow, I thought.

THE NEXT DAY MY LANDLORD-AND-TENANT CALENDAR was especially heavy, including an unexpected trial, and I didn't get into the office until late afternoon. I caught the boss just as the big man was about to leave. "Make it quick, kid. It's Kathy's birthday and I promised to take her out to dinner."

After hearing me out, Rooney scratched his head. "It's a bitch. I'd really like to stay the hell away from those bums, but the ostrich defense isn't a good idea. We need to know what they have in mind. Have that drink with Flynn, and see what he has to say, but make no decisions without consulting with me, and that doesn't mean just a phone call.

And don't delay the meeting, make it tonight or tomorrow at the latest."

EARLY THE NEXT EVENING, I ENTERED O'NEILS'S. It was a cleaner version of the Irish bars in the Bronx where I'd lifted a few with my then boss, Judge McCann. The long bar to the left of the door was mostly occupied by a noisy crowd of after-work revelers. I scrutinized the bar but didn't see my host. I was about to ask the red-bearded bartender when I heard my name called and glancing to the right I saw Flynn seated at the table furthest from the door. "Hi, Al," I said as I reached the table.

Flynn emptied his glass and placed it beside an empty one with melting ice. "Thanks for coming, Ian. What're you drinking?"

"Scotch on the rocks would be fine."

"Dewars?"

I nodded and Flynn held up four fingers to the bartender. When the drinks came, he tossed off half of his in a single swallow. "So how's it going?"

"I'm getting by." I sipped my scotch.

Flynn finished his first drink, pushed it aside, wrapped his hand around the second glass, and opened his mouth to speak but froze.

"What's the matter, Al?"

"Nothing." Flynn shook his head. "That's not so. The

new will case is dragging. Nobody believes us, and—" he hesitated— "and Alice and I feel bad about how we treated you."

You should, I thought, but held my tongue. Then I heard the first six notes of "When Irish Eyes Are Smiling" emanating from my companion.

Flynn pulled a cell phone from his inside jacket pocket. pressed a button, listened, said, "Yes," hung up, and returned it to his pocket.

"What was that?"

"You'll see." Flynn took a long pull on his drink and held up two fingers.

We drank silently until the refill arrived. As the bartender turned to leave, I heard a familiar woman's voice. "Kevin, I'll take a double Bushmills on ice," said Alice Keller as she seated herself between us. She opened the buttons on her coat and flipped it over the back of her chair, revealing an attractive blue silk dress. She presented her cheeks for the obligatory kiss by each of her male companions. "Surprised to see me, Ian?"

"A little."

"I guess nothing I do surprises you."

I nodded.

When her Irish arrived, she sipped slowly for a few minutes. "This smooth-talking Irishman is showing signs of embarrassment, and wanted his mommy to talk for him."

Flynn nodded.

"Let me fill you in on what's going on." She took another sip of her drink. "The night of our hospital fiasco, I was sitting in the office going over old files when, lo and behold, I came up with a folder I hadn't seen before. In it was a will of my uncle." She reached into her pocketbook, pulled out an envelope, and handed it to me. "This is a copy."

I skimmed it.

"I wasn't sure what to do, so I called Al."

"Why Al? I was your lawyer."

"I don't know. I think I was angry at you over the hospital thing."

"What'd *I* do?"

"Nothing. I had to be mad at somebody, and I picked you. Anyway, I called Al and read it to him."

"And I came up to the office," Al said.

A great act, I thought, wondering if they'd rehearsed it between the sheets.

"And when I looked at the will, I noticed that it had been witnessed by two law school classmates who died at the World Trade Center."

"What an *amazing* coincidence," I said.

"In any event, I've got to testify about their signatures."

"How come you know their handwriting?" I asked, pretending to go along.

"We were in the same fraternity, and I was the secretary."

"Very interesting. What's it got to do with me?"

Flynn finished his remaining drink and signaled the bartender. "Well, you know I can't testify and be the lawyer, so Alice and I want you to represent her in the new case."

"What about your firm?"

"They don't want to touch it. Said to get someone else."

"Will you do it?" she asked.

"Why me, Alice? After—"

She held up her hand. "Don't say it. I know what I did ,and I'm sorry. Please help me. I promise you'll be paid."

"What about the old case?"

"That, too."

I expelled air. "I don't know. I've got to discuss it with my boss."

"Call him now?" said Flynn taking out his cell.

I shook my head. "No. It's got to be face to face." I left ten minutes later, promising to give Flynn my answer the next day.

I MET ROONEY FOR BREAKFAST, before court, at the deli across the street from the courthouse.

"How'd it go?" the big man asked between mouthfuls of bacon, eggs, and fries.

I filled him in.

Rooney was in deep concentration as he emptied his plate. Then he swallowed a mouthful of coffee and shook his head. "No way. Tell Flynn no deal. This thing stinks to high heaven, and I don't want you losing your license over it."

I called Flynn's cell phone before court and left a call-back message on his voice mail. When I returned to the office I had a message that Flynn had called. I immediately returned the call and Flynn picked up on the first ring. "Hi, Al."

"Hi. What's the answer?"

"Sorry. We can't do it."

"I expected that. I'll tell Alice."

Ten minutes later, there was a buzz on the intercom. "Yes, Rosie."

"Alice Keller is on the line."

"Hi, Alice. I'm sorry I—"

"You fucking son-of-a-bitch. I'll make sorry you were ever born." She hung up before I could reply.

CHAPTER TWENTY-SIX

WHEN I GOT TO THE OFFICE A WEEK LATER, I stopped at the front desk and saw that I had received a phone message. "Rosie, who's Jason Kelly?"

"Beats me, Mr. Elkins. The only thing he said was he was in from out of town and wants to talk to you on a matter you're handling. He said he'd call again."

Half an hour later, I was finishing an egg salad sandwich at my desk when the intercom buzzed.

"You have a long-distance call from Sister Mary Elizabeth Curran. Have you finally seen the light and plan on coming over to our church?"

"I'll think about it, Rosie. Put her on."

"Mr. Elkins?"

"Yes, Sister. How are you?"

"Quite well, thank you. Have you spoken to my attorney?"

"Is that Jason Kelly?"

"Yes."

"He's called, but so far we're playing telephone tag. What's it about?"

"My Uncle Jim's will."

"The one your Cousin Alice found? I'm not representing her anymore. You might want to speak to Al Flynn."

"No, not that one—and I *don't* like Mr. Flynn."

"I can't say I'm enamored of him either. What will *do* you mean?"

"I think I'd like Mr. Kelly to tell you about it. When you speak to him, ask him to call me."

The office phone rang just as I was leaving. Since Rosie had long since gone, I picked up. It was Jason Kelly, who added, after he introduced himself, "I'm a Texas lawyer."

"So I've heard. Sister Mary Elizabeth wants you to call her."

"I will, tonight. I just got into Kennedy, and I'd like to talk to you."

"I assume this is about McGrath."

"That's right. "

"I may not be able to. You know Alice Keller was my

client."

"I'm sure that what I want to talk about won't present an ethical problem. I certainly don't expect you to breach confidentiality. When can I see you?"

"I'm in court tomorrow morning, but I expect to be back in the office by the middle of the afternoon. Do you need directions?"

"No problem, I'm an ex-Bronxite. I'll be there at three."

True to his word, Kelly was seated in the waiting area when I returned from court.

"How do you take your coffee?"

"Black with one sugar."

"We'll be in the library, Rosie."

"I'll bring the coffee right in. Would you like some of Mr. Rooney's goodies? He's been sneaking them in again."

"Are you a cake eater, Jason? My boss is a gourmand in that department."

"I used to be before I had to shrink back into this suit."

"My boss tried that for a few weeks, but he's at the old stand again. Just coffee, thanks, Rosie."

When we had settled down in the library, Kelly opened his tan leather attaché case and took out a file. "Have you seen Alice's new will, Ian?"

"Your coffee, gentlemen," Rosie announced as she set down two containers, "and you might want to try these," she added, putting down a paper plate with some white cookies. "They have no sugar and very few calories." She left the room.

"Yes, Al Flynn showed it to me a week ago, and he tried to get me to represent Alice Keller in proving it."

"Are you?"

"No, we decided against it."

Kelly breathed a sigh of relief. "Is this the one?" he asked, handing over a photocopy.

"That's the one," I replied. The document was dated later than Alice's first attempt. The cover read *Keen & O'Hara, Counselors At Law*. It left a third of the estate to Alice and her sister, and two-thirds to "The Convent of the Sacred Heart of Houston, Texas, in fulfillment of my promise to my dear sister, Mary Curran, and her daughter, Sister Mary Elizabeth." Alice was named as executrix.

"I assume you know the lawyers are dead."

Kelly nodded. "The Department of State confirmed there was no listing for them, and they told me that the registration number on the notary stamp had never been issued. You should be glad you didn't take the case."

"Very interesting. How do you think I can help you?"

"I'm not really sure. Frankly, if I didn't know something about you, I probably wouldn't have called."

"You don't say."

Kelly chuckled and took a sip of coffee. "I'm sorry to

seem mysterious. We have a mutual friend—you know Ted McGuire?"

"Sure. I used to work with Ted. He broke me in when I first joined the surrogate's court. He left the office about a year after I got there. I think he's up for partner in one of the big shops. How do you know him?"

"He's my big brother's closest friend—best man at Joe's wedding. Senior at law school when I was a freshman. Ted's one hell of a guy."

"He sure is. How is he?"

"Very well. I'm having dinner with him tonight."

"Send him my best."

"I will. He thinks very highly of you. Tells me you're not only a good lawyer, but a genuine straight shooter, which is why I wanted to talk to you, and why I'm going to fill you in on some details."

"I'm all ears."

"Near the end of the trial, my client received a phone call from a Mr. Isadore Finkelstein, who said he was a retired lawyer."

"He was with Cohen and Finkelstein. They did the Bronx dispossesses for McGrath."

"That's right. He told the sister that he had done a will and a codicil for Mr. McGrath, and that the convent was the chief beneficiary."

I picked up one of the cookies, turned it in my hand,

and returned it to the plate. "How come he waited so long to come forward?"

Kelly smiled. "They're an addiction," he said pointing to the plate. "Finkelstein retired to Florida a few years ago and hadn't heard about McGrath's death. When he came up here for a visit, his former partner told him about it."

"That's strange—I spoke to Cohen right after I was retained, and he didn't know about any will."

"Finkelstein told me that his will business was a sideline, and that he didn't split with his partner."

"Have you seen this will and codicil?"

"Not yet, but he told me that the will leaves a hundred grand to Charles McGrath and everything else to the convent."

"What about the codicil?"

"He did the codicil right before he retired to Florida. McGrath apparently caught his brother taking kickbacks from contractors, fired him, and made his niece, Alice, his manager. The codicil revokes the bequest to Charlie and makes a $50,000.00 one to Alice. I guess, if he'd lived, he might have upped that to $100,000.00."

"Who's the executor?"

"Finkelstein."

"I guess he'll do the legal work."

"No, he's retired."

"Will he give it to Cohen?"

"Nope. When Cohen told him about McGrath's death, he let slip about his moonlighting. Cohen had a shit fit, and they're not on speaking terms. That's why I'm here."

"I'd love to handle it, but I'd have a conflict with Alice. What about Flynn's firm? They represent the cardinal."

"I don't trust him. He was a smiling snake when we were in law school together, and that will he came up with stinks to high heaven. Besides, he has the same conflict with Alice that you have. What I'd like from you is some help in finding the right lawyer."

I pondered for a moment, then smiled. "Let me talk to my boss first. One of my closest friends has an uncle who practices up in Westchester named Mike Crowley. Good lawyer, and he's done probate litigation. I think he'd be ideal."

The young Texan nodded. "He might be just the right man for the job. No offense, Ian, but I believe that our archbishop would be more comfortable with a Crowley than a Cohen."

BY THE MIDDLE OF NOVEMBER, INDIAN SUMMEr had just ended. There was a chill in the air as I covered the three blocks from my office to the courthouse. When I returned at noon, I found a message that Bill Anderson, the chief law assistant, wanted to see me at three. I wondered whether I was in trouble again. "Come in," Anderson called out in response to my knock.

"Hi, Bill. You wanted to see me?"

He was seated behind his cluttered desk. "Under other circumstances, I'd offer you a seat but. . ." He pointed to his visitors chairs. Two were stacked with files, the third occupied by Herb Crowley.

"You mean I have to stand when I face the firing squad?"

"He thinks he's only in a little trouble," Crowley quipped.

"Yeah, wait till he finds out," Anderson added, rising from his seat. "The boss wants to see you."

We trooped through the door leading into the judge's library. Judge Stevens was seated behind his desk, reading a memo. His jacket was draped over the back of his chair and his blue checked vest was open. "He's here, Judge," Anderson announced.

"Good to see you," the judge said as he rose to greet and shake my hand. "Thanks for coming over."

"My pleasure, Your Honor."

"Have a seat," Stevens said, motioning. "There's something I want to discuss with you fellows." As we took seats, the judge pressed the intercom. "Nelda, will you please bring us a pot of your delicious coffee and four cups."

"Coming right up, Your Honor. Want some cookies?"

Stevens glanced at us and we all shook our heads. "No,

thanks, just coffee." There was just small talk until the restorative arrived; then the judge said, "I guess you're wondering why I asked you here, Ian."

"Actually, I thought it was Bill who was calling me on the carpet."

The judge chuckled. "I assume you've heard about Joe Medina."

I nodded. "Damn shame. Just elected to his first term in congress, and he has a heart attack and dies"

"It sure is," Stevens agreed. "On the other hand, it makes for interesting possibilities. . . . There'll be a special election in January. I've spoken to the county chairman, and I can have the nomination if I want it."

"Wouldn't that be a step backwards, Judge?"

"I don't think so. I should never have taken *this* job. It doesn't fit my temperament. I liked it a lot better when I was in the legislature, and I think I'd have more of a future in Congress. I could even be put up for a national office. If I stay here, maybe I could get to the Court of Appeals."

"If that's what you want, I'd be pleased to work for your election," I replied.

"That's what I hoped you'd say, and I definitely want you on my election committee. You did a great job for Bill when he ran against me, and I sure can use you. Of course, once I'm nominated, I'll have to step down from the bench. One of the Supreme Court judges will fill in for me, and Bill and Herb will, of course, stay in their jobs until then. The county chairman has assured me that Bill will be nominated to succeed me as surrogate. I don't know what the temporary surrogate will do for you, but I'm sure Bill will either take you back into the law department or give you plenty of appointments when he gets my spot. In the meantime, my friend Al Carter has told me that he was greatly impressed with you and has good things for you. He'll also spread your name around to the other area surrogates."

"Judge, I certainly appreciate what you're doing for me, and you know you can count on me for anything I can do for you."

Stevens nodded. "By the way, your good friend has some interesting news for you."

Herb Crowley put down his cup. "Uncle Mike's brought me up to date on the McGrath estate. He says that he pressured Flynn's firm to drop his phony will and settle with the two brothers."

"What did they get?"

"A hundred thousand each, plus their legals will be picked up by the estate. Alice Keller gets nothing, but her legals also come out of the estate."

"Why would she agree to that? She did better with the deal I made with the convent for her through Flynn and under the legitimate will."

"She argued that, but they had the goods on her. It

seems that Jay Kelly was talking with Alice's two witnesses. They're real pissed off at her and let on about a certain conspiracy to probate a phony will. Uncle Mike convinced her that if she didn't take the deal she'd probably be prosecuted and do some jail time. Your friend Flynn didn't do as well. Judge Carter reported the problem to the Second Department Grievance Committee. Flynn's firm fired him, and he's probably up for disbarment."

I shook my head. "I should have known."

"There's something in it for your firm, too."

"Oh?"

"Yes. Your legals will also come out of the estate. You'll be getting a decision from Judge Carter ordering you to submit an affidavit of your services."

"I trust your Uncle Mike did okay."

"He'll get good legals, but even better than that, the Houston archbishop spoke to the cardinal. Flynn's firm is out, and Uncle Mike will be getting some of the archdiocese's work. I think he's going to be talking to your boss about a merger of your firms. He thinks it could be beneficial to both, and who knows—there might even be something in it for you."